Storm
a novel

Other Books In the Soul Surfer Series:

Soul Surfer Bible

Fiction:
Clash (Book One)
Burned (Book Two)
Crunch (Book Four)

Nonfiction:
Ask Bethany—FAQs: Surfing, Faith & Friends
Rise Above: A 90-Day Devotional

a novel

By Rick Bundschuh
Inspired by Bethany Hamilton

zonder**kidz**

ZONDERVAN.com/
AUTHORTRACKER
follow your favorite authors

zonderkidz.
The children's group of Zondervan

www.zonderkidz.com

Storm
Copyright © 2007 by Bethany Hamilton

Requests for information should be addressed to:
Grand Rapids, Michigan 49530

ISBN-10: 0-310-71224-6
ISBN-13: 978-0-310-71224-4

CIP Applied for

Editor: Barbara Scott
Art direction: Merit Alderink
Interior composition: Christine Orejuela-Winkelman
Illustrations: Monika Roe
Photography: Noah Hamilton

Printed in the United States of America

07 08 09 10 • 10 9 8 7 6 5 4 3 2 1

Introduction

Bethany Hamilton is more than a great surfer; she is a great athlete. Surfing just happens to be her sport of choice. Watching her in action, I am sure she would excel at just about anything she set her heart on.

Like most terrific athletes, Bethany has natural talent. But in addition to that, she also trains hard, is careful about what she eats, and often pushes herself physically past the comfort zone of most people.

The idea for this story actually came from listening to Bethany talk ever so casually to some of her friends about running in one of the remote valleys that hug the towering cliffs on Kauai's north shore ... for fun.

Now for most people, the trek that she mentioned as if it were a stroll in the park is a pretty tough little hike over uneven ground with not a handrail in sight to keep the careless from plunging over a thousand-foot cliff.

And it can be treacherous. People do get in trouble on that same hike that Bethany sometimes uses as a training ground. Some of those people are experience hikers, some are merely foolish.

This story is also about surprises.

A typical uneventful day can suddenly turn out to be an adventure. A simple kind gesture can set in motion a chain of blessings much bigger than we could ever have imagined.

God especially likes to surprise us by showing up just when he is needed most.

It is often when life turns from easy to extreme that we find the limits of our own abilities ... and the unlimited love, strength, and power of God.

Now you may not be a natural athlete like Bethany, but it is my prayer that her grit, self-discipline, and determination might encourage you to push harder to be better at whatever good thing you set your mind to do.

And see if God doesn't throw a few of his surprises in for you at the same time.

Rick Bundschuh
Kauai, Hawaii

Prologue

How did it get dark so quickly? It was way too dark ...

So dark that Bethany had no idea she was falling until she felt the wind rushing through her long blonde hair—felt the sudden odd weightless sensation envelop her like the floor dropping out from underneath her on one of the crazy amusement park rides that she and her brothers loved to go on.

Except she didn't exactly feel like laughing and screaming her guts out. Well, screaming, maybe. But not laughing. At least not yet ...

Her back suddenly slapped against water. Natural instinct immediately took over, and she began to scissor her legs back and forth, treading the cold water as she squinted through the dark to get her bearings.

Tiny flashes of lightning flickered, glancing off the waves rolling and surging around her. *Big waves*, she thought grimly. *The kind of huge swells you get in a bad storm.* As soon as she had that thought, the sound of thunder boomed overhead and a heavy, windswept rain began to fall around her.

Bethany felt a shiver of fear as she tried to blink the rain out of her eyes. Then, as her vision cleared, she spotted a large outcropping of rock a short distance away, and her fear was quickly replaced with determination. She began to swim for the rock.

You can do this, Hamilton!

Bethany gritted her teeth and focused on the strength of her right arm and her legs to propel her through the choppy water. She reminded herself of the hours spent with the swim team—on the workouts that she had developed to strengthen every muscle.

Come on! You've trained for times like this!

A huge wave rolled over her, but she pushed the panic aside as she struggled to keep her nose and mouth above the water. Her teeth chattered. *No time for freaking out!* She waited for a lull between waves and craned her neck to catch a glimpse of the rock. She was over halfway there.

Just a little farther . . .

Bethany kicked her legs for all she was worth, using her right arm in a powerful side stroke that she had developed not long after she'd lost her arm . . . and then she felt something brush past her leg.

Shark! She squeezed her eyes shut, willing herself not to think about the attack—not to think about what might be in the water with her right now—and continued to swim. The waves were growing larger and stronger, and in spite of all of her training, she felt the last of her strength being sucked out of her. For the first time since the whole nightmare started, she wondered if she was going to make it.

Please, God . . .

Suddenly she felt the edge of the rock scrape against her hand. A dizzying kind of relief washed over her, giving her just enough strength to grab on to the rock with one arm as she pulled herself out of the water.

Weak and shivering like crazy, Bethany barely managed to drag herself up on the rock. Even through the thick sheet of rain, she could see that her arm and legs were majorly banged up, but she felt herself grin in spite of it all as she looked to the sky. The black storm clouds were retreating, and she could see a glimpse of sunshine breaking through. She struggled to a sitting position, wet and still shivering but never so happy in her life to see the sun.

Bethany brushed her hair out of her eyes and scanned the horizon hopefully for someone—anyone—that could help her. There was no one. Nothing but dark crashing waves of water as far as her eyes could see.

I'm alone.

The wind and rain abruptly disappeared, as if they were sucked away by a huge vacuum. Everything went still. She looked around, not really sure what was happening, when she felt a warm, syrupy feeling wash over her. The kind of feeling she got when she fell asleep between her mom and dad on the couch while watching TV. Protected. Like everything was okay.

Bethany bolted awake and looked around. Surf posters glinted in the moonlight. Swimsuits draped over the back of a chair. A Switchfoot CD lay open on the floor. She wasn't in the middle of an ocean. She was ... *home*. She breathed a huge sigh of relief and flopped back against her pillow.

Just a dream.

one

"My lungs are going to collapse!" Holly Silva gasped as she melted into a human puddle on the park grass. "I can't believe you talked me into this!"

"You're welcome," Bethany panted as she landed next to Holly with a grin. She never got tired of running at Hanalei Bay. Surrounded by towering green cliffs and waterfalls that seemed to go on forever, it was like having a running trail in the middle of Jurassic Park. Minus the man-eating dinosaurs, of course.

The run had been good for her, she thought, glancing up at the wide blue bowl of sky. Good enough to shake off the cloud that had been looming over her ever since waking from that crazy dream.

"How many miles was that?"

Bethany glanced over as Holly threw her arms wide across the grass. Bethany smiled. The cool thing about hanging with Holly was you couldn't stay in a weird mood for long.

"Miles? More like one mile," Bethany said, and then laughed as Holly's green eyes widened in disbelief. "It's running in the sand that gets you."

"It's running in the sand *after* surfing all morning. No wonder Malia and Jenna bailed on us!"

"Malia and Jenna aren't as gullible as you," Bethany teased. Bethany had to bite her lip to keep from giggling as her friend sat up. Holly's short brown hair was dark with sweat and sticking up all over the place.

"It's winter training, Holly," Bethany continued when she was able to talk without laughing. "You'll be glad you did it with me when you survive Hanalei Bay when it's fifteen feet."

"News flash, Bethany; I don't like to surf when it's fifteen feet—*you* like to surf when it's fifteen feet!" Holly narrowed her eyes. "And why do you keep looking at my hair?"

"Well ..." Bethany burst out laughing. "It's a little scary."

"Ugh," Holly groaned, running her hands through her hair as her eyes darted toward the cute surfers tossing a Frisbee on the beach. "That's what I get for following you around the bay twice!"

Bethany smiled as she turned her gaze towards the rocky shoreline on the other side of the bay. Suddenly, her smile faded a little and she felt a shiver go up her back. Why couldn't she shake that dream? *There was something about those rocks—*

"So, tell me why you like torturing yourself like this." Holly said, interrupting Bethany's thoughts.

Bethany leaned back in the grass and thought for a moment. "Remember last January at the Big Surf?"

"I remember you were the only girl crazy enough to go out."

"Well, I got caught by flat rock in a cleanup set. I was pinned to the bottom for the first wave, rolled around by the second, and finally broke surface for a breath after the third wave—"

"Exactly *why* I don't surf the bay when it's fifteen feet!"

"No, you don't get it! What I'm saying is, I was a little freaked out—but not like I would've been if I hadn't trained. If you *know* you can handle a couple of wave hold downs, then it isn't as scary ..." Bethany's voice trailed off as she thought about the dream again, and she wondered if it meant that she needed to train harder—be better prepared.

She glanced over at Holly who was quiet for once, with a thoughtful look on her face as she studied the sky. Bethany wished Holly would say something—anything—to lighten the mood.

"Hello?"

"I was just trying to figure out what's worse," Holly said finally, her grin reappearing. "Training with you or being wiped out by a massive wave."

"Very funny."

"I gotta get up and find something to drink," Holly said with a laugh, then groaned as she slowly rose to her feet. "My body hates me, and we still have the car wash to do!"

"Let's head into town. I'll buy you a bottle of water for being such a good sport," Bethany offered.

Holly arched a brow at her. "Good sport?"

"Okay ... for running with me!" Bethany added. They both laughed.

"Ready to stagger to the store?" asked Holly.

"You stagger—I kinda feel like jogging."

"Bethany, you are such a show-off!"

Bethany grinned, feeling her spirits rise. "Catch up, and I'll let you in on an idea I have for the car wash!"

"I'm probably going to regret this!" Holly called out and then ran to catch up.

They were guzzling water in front of the Big Save grocery store when Bethany's mom arrived to shuttle them to the church car wash.

"I don't know how you girls do it," Cheri said as they scrambled into the van. "I have a hard time keeping up as the driver!"

"You reap what you sow, Mom. Isn't that what you always tell me?"

"Hmm." Cheri pursed her lips in thought as she backed out of the parking space. "I wonder what the wash-me bandits are going to reap?"

She grinned at Holly in the rearview mirror. "Any ideas?"

Holly blushed, but Bethany burst out laughing. Her mom had spotted all the dirty rear windows they had written *wash me* on as they headed into town.

"We'll reap business for the car wash—for the mission trip."

"So we can go build homes in Mexico for those less fortunate." Holly added with a hopeful grin.

"Uh, huh," Cheri said, and then did a double take in the rearview mirror. "Okay, how did you two manage to get *my* back window without me noticing?"

Cheri shook her head in amazement, and Bethany and Holly broke into a fresh round of laughter.

"Is this the third or fourth car wash?" Holly asked once she caught her breath.

"Third," Bethany said, glancing over the seat. "I just wish there was something else we could do. It feels like it's taking forever, and I've been dying to go on a mission trip since I was little!"

"Too bad we're not *trustafarians*."

"What?" Bethany and her mom said at the same time and then laughed.

Holly grinned. "You know, hippies with Rastafarian hair who live in the jungle and only come into town to get money out of their trustfund accounts. *Trust-afarians*. Get it?"

Bethany and her mom groaned. Holly was almost famous for the crazy way she described people. If she didn't know of a term, she was happy to make one up.

"Check it out," Holly said, suddenly pointing to the side passenger window. Bethany turned in time to see a long black limousine in the lane next to them. "*They* should be at our fundraiser!"

"No doubt," Bethany said slowly as she watched the limo pick up speed to pass them. She was suddenly caught off guard as the face of a teenage girl turned to stare back at them. She was pretty in a polished kind of way, with dark hair cut in a shiny bob and fair skin. The girl noticed them watching her and quickly looked away.

"Probably a *celebutante*," Holly added knowingly.

Bethany grinned and shook her head just as the girl glanced up to the sky. Bethany was struck hard by the sad look on the girl's face.

I wonder what it is that's made her so sad?

Something about the girl tugged at Bethany — something she couldn't put her finger on — like the way her eyes kept being drawn back to the rocks at Hanalei Bay. Like her dream.

It wasn't that she thought people with money couldn't have problems. Her friend Liam and his dad had been through some really bad stuff — until they found God. Even now, they still dealt with the same things everyone worried and prayed about. But what if someone didn't know God? What if what they owned was all they thought they had?

"Is that it?" Andrea looked out the window of the limousine to the west as an awesome view of towering cliffs with waterfalls free-falling down to a slip of white sand and ocean opened up before them. Colorado had some cool-looking mountains, she thought, but *nothing* like this.

"Yeah, that's it, kiddo."

Andrea turned around, surprised at the hint of excitement she thought she heard in her mom's voice. Her mom glanced up from the map she'd been squinting at and smiled—a smile that Andrea couldn't ever remember seeing before. For a moment, she almost looked and sounded kind of young.

Maybe. She tried not to hope too much, but she yearned to have a real family that hung out together. She thought of the blonde girl she'd seen in the van, hair blowing in the wind, with such a huge smile on her face. The lady driving had the same kind of smile. They looked like they were having fun together.

Andrea looked across the seat to where her dad sat. She saw that he was looking toward the cliffs too. She almost reached out to grab his hand.

Something about the way he looked reminded her of herself; sad and alone, even in a car full of people. *I wonder if he's thinking about Uncle Mike?*

Andrea glanced at her brother. He was sprawled out on the seat next to her as he nodded along with whatever was playing on his iPod. Mark drove her crazy most of the time, but she couldn't imagine what it would be like without him. "One day he's there, and the next he's just ... gone," she'd heard her dad say with a shaky voice the night he got the call about Uncle Mike.

He'd said it like it couldn't be real. It wasn't real to her, either. Her uncle was gone. Gone where?

Andrea leaned her head against the car window and glanced up to the blue expanse of sky again, searching. She'd never really thought about that kind of stuff until now—she knew for sure her mom and dad hadn't.

Her dad's mantra had always been if something was lost or broken, you opened your wallet and bought a replacement—or had it fixed.

But people can't be replaced, Andrea thought, curling her legs under her as she stared at the sky. And she'd never heard of anyone that could fix a broken heart.

two

"Pretty awesome to see God pulling all of these teenagers together for a good cause," Cheri said, sharing a smile with Bethany as she steered the van around the bustling lot of people where the car wash was going to be held. Hoses were coiled in the far corner of the shopping center. Buckets and large bottles of soap were lined up on the curb like soldiers waiting for orders. Two girls from the Hanalei Girls Surf Team looked over, waved to Bethany and Holly, and then grabbed up their sponges, buckets, and hoses and headed their way.

"Want your car washed, Mom?" Bethany asked with a Cheshire-cat grin.

"I always want my car washed. Thank you, Bethany!"

"Okay, get your money ready."

"Hmm ... I thought you'd give me a freebie for being your surf taxi."

"Well, today you've gotta pay!"

"Oh, that's right. It's mom slash surf taxi slash *wallet*!" Cheri said, and Bethany and Holly laughed.

"Here's the first customer!" Bethany called, hanging her head out the window of the van. Within an instant, the dirty, surf-wax-stained van was attacked from all sides in a flurry of water, suds, and sponges.

"Love ya, Mom!" Bethany laughed as she scrambled from the van.

"We'll wash your car one of these days for free, Auntie Cheri," Holly added with a benevolent smile before she shut the door.

Within seconds, Bethany and Holly were joined by Malia, Jenna, and Monica as they made a bee-line for Sarah, the youth director of North Shore Christian Church.

As usual, Sarah was in her element, directing from her small plastic table with a water bottle in one hand and a yellow notepad in the other. Her blonde hair was pulled back in a neat ponytail, and her makeup was perfect—in spite of the fact that she would be in the hot sun, spraying cars down all day.

"A girl after my own heart. Look at how perfect her face looks," Holly said with a sigh, and the girls all laughed. In addition to creating new ways to describe people, Holly was also known for her love of all things girlie. Makeup was a new love, but it had a powerful pull, mainly because Holly's mom wouldn't let her wear it.

"So, how was the run, Holly?" Malia asked sweetly.

But then, Malia was sweet.

Holly narrowed her eyes anyway. "My heart nearly exploded—not that you or Jenna would care."

Bethany, Jenna, and Malia burst out laughing. Holly grinned.

"I could've warned you about Bethany, but no one listens to me anyway," Monica sniffed. "I know how people respond to my advice. Oh, sure! Why don't we add the whole *island* to the surf team, Monica?"

"Oh, cut it out, Monica. I've been on the team for over a year now. You need to find something else to gripe about," Jenna blurted out, then blushed to the almost exact shade of her red hair. Everyone fell silent.

They could all remember when Monica had been reluctant to invite Jenna onto the Hanalei Girls Surf Team last year.

Bethany grinned.

"Impressive," Monica said, not knowing what else to say, and they all laughed, including Monica.

"Okay, surf girls," Sarah announced, breaking into their banter. "Step up and be counted!" She checked their names off her list and looked up with a grin. "Growth spurt! Bethany, you are definitely roof girl today."

The other girls snickered.

"Better than hubcap girls," Bethany said, sliding a grin at Holly and Malia, the shortest of their group.

Cars were lining up now, and as soon as Sarah checked off the last girl, she left her little table to act as traffic director, greeter, and cashier.

More students arrived and joined in the work. Many, not waiting to get orders from Sarah, simply picked up a sponge, commandeered a hose, or grabbed a chamois. They all worked well together too — for most of the day.

Then there was the little incident of turning the hoses on each other that became an awesome eruption of flying sponges filled with soap and spraying water. Sarah managed to bring everything back under control until the end when Bethany, Holly, and a couple of the boys gave her the "grand finale" by dumping a bucket of water over her head.

Sarah took the dousing in good humor, cheerfully threatening revenge on the plotters.

"I wouldn't take it so well if I got my makeup messed up like that," Holly noted gravely as she and Bethany emptied buckets and rung out sponges.

"Holly, you're starting to scare me," Bethany teased as they made their way back to where Sarah sat. They plopped down next to Sarah as she counted the money for the mission trip.

"So, how did we do?" Bethany asked hopefully.

"Not too bad," Sarah said with an encouraging smile. "We're a couple hundred closer to our goal."

"How much more do we need?" Holly asked.

"I figure around five thousand dollars," Sarah said.

"Why so much?" Bethany asked, trying not to let her heart sink.

"Well, we need to rent vans, pay for lodging, and help with airfare. And then there is the cost of the materials to build the houses in Mexico," Sarah said, and then smiled. "The only thing that comes cheap on this whole trip is our labor."

"Too bad the celebutante didn't show up today," Holly sniffed. "If I were rich, I'd fund the whole mission trip!"

Yeah, Bethany thought, ready to climb aboard Holly's pity train ... until she saw the crooked smile on Sarah's face.

"You two need to quit worrying about what other people have and trust God," Sarah said as she packed her things away. "We're talking about *God*. You know, Creator of the universe! Don't you think he can get the money to us for this little mission trip?"

"Well, why hasn't he then?" Bethany asked, then bit her lip worriedly. "I mean, I don't mean to sound disrespectful or anything ..."

"I don't get it, either," Holly admitted. "We're trying to do something good—something I really think God wants done—but it's been really hard for us to make the money to cover everything. Then there's my uncle who goes to Vegas to drink, party, and gamble ... and he comes home with twenty grand in his pocket!" Holly bit her lip too. Then, unable to stop herself, she added, "What's up with that?"

Sarah nodded thoughtfully. "First thing I want to say is that it's cool you two are asking questions. Second thing is, God always answers—even his silence can be an answer."

Bethany figured she and Holly must have had some strange looks on their faces, because Sarah looked at them and laughed.

"Remember the book we read about the woman who was in the concentration camp with her sister?"

"Corrie ten Boom?" Bethany said.

Sarah nodded. "Yeah, that's her. There were many times when she felt like God was silent. But she eventually learned that if she just kept trusting him, kept marching forward, he would see her through and provide what she needed—exactly when she needed it.

"She liked to tell the story about her father putting her on the train to visit her grandparents as a little girl—how she was so scared to make the journey alone. She said her dad would walk her to the train, help her get seated, and then silently wait to make sure she was really ready—that she could handle the trip—then he would finally hand her the ticket for her journey.

"After she was released from the concentration camp, she lived the rest of her life that way; believing that if it was God's will, he would provide. You see, Corrie learned that when we are weak, God works through us. He is strong *in us*."

"That's pretty cool," Bethany said.

"Must've been pretty hard too," Holly added.

"You never know how or when he's going to work it all out," Sarah said. "But that's the fun part."

"Fun?" Bethany and Holly said at the same time, and they all laughed.

"Yeah, fun!" Sarah said. "Think of it as an awesome mystery, and God leaves you clues to follow along the way." Sarah chuckled. "Sometimes you don't even realize they are clues until the end of the mystery."

With the parking lot now empty, the girls helped Sarah pack up her car. Sarah offered to treat the girls to smoothies and then give them a ride home.

Bethany was strapping herself into the front passenger seat, thinking hard about their conversation, when an idea suddenly popped into her head. *Thanks, Liam!*

"Sarah, do you think we could maybe do something other than a car wash?"

"I suppose so. What do you have in mind?"

"It may be a dumb idea."

"Try me!"

"Well, do you know what a jog-a-thon is?"

Holly let out an audible groan from the backseat, causing Bethany to grin.

"Yep," Sarah nodded. "You get sponsors to pledge money for every mile you run."

"Well, I was thinking that maybe we could have a *surf-a-thon*. Kind of like a jog-a-thon, but where people commit money to every wave ridden to the beach."

"Hmmm." Sarah cocked her head to one side, thinking. "It has possibilities. But don't you think it would be hard to get people to pledge for something that is so much fun? And what about the kids in our youth group who don't surf?"

"I was just thinking about that," Bethany said, trying to contain her excitement. "Maybe this is stupid, but what if we had a surf-a-thon with inflatable pool toys? You know, those big blow-up animals, air mattresses, and inner tubes."

Sarah's eyes danced at the idea.

"Sounds crazy," Holly said from the backseat. But when Bethany turned around, she could see Holly was just teasing her.

"If it was crazy *enough*, people might be interested in supporting it!" Bethany rushed on. "And you don't need to know how to surf to ride one of those things to the beach; all you have to do is to hang on!"

"You know, I think you might be on to something," Sarah said.

"It would be a lot more fun than another car wash," Holly added, catching the excitement.

"Well, I think we may have a few more of those in our future. But the surf-a-thon sounds like a really unique way to have fun *and* to help us raise funds."

"I vote for the surf-a-thon" Holly said.

"I thought you wanted the jog-a-thon," Bethany said, trying to sound innocent.

Holly's heavy silence was followed by a burst of laughter from all three of them as Sarah popped the girls' favorite Switchfoot CD into her player. There was no mention of running or anything else until they stopped and parked next to Hanalei Harry's Smoothie Shack.

After they ordered their smoothies, Bethany, Holly, and Sarah sat down at a bench together to sip their drinks. Bethany stirred her papaya and acai fruit smoothie with a straw and thought about the surf-a-thon idea.

"Check it out," Holly said, tapping Bethany's shoulder as she pointed. "It's the celebutante and her mom!"

Bethany glanced over to see the teenage girl they had seen riding in the limo earlier that day. She and her mom were sitting at a picnic table, drinking smoothies, and looking at a Kauai hiking trails book. Bethany overheard the girl mention the Hanakapiai Trail.

"Sounds like they're going for a hike," Bethany said. "Hey, Holly, why don't we run the Hanakapiai Trail tomorrow."

"Ugh!"

"Come on, it'll be fun," Bethany coaxed. "We can run to the stream, go bodysurfing, and then run back."

Holly pursed her lips as she thought it over. "Well, I guess I could. If it's good enough for the celebutante, it's good enough for me."

"Thatta girl!" Bethany laughed.

"Do you know that girl?" Sarah asked.

"No, she's just some rich girl we saw riding in a limo earlier," Holly said with a disdainful note to her voice. Sarah raised her eyebrows at her.

"I know your parents didn't teach either of you to think of people like that!"

"I know, I know," Holly said as Bethany glanced back at her with a sheepish look.

"Well," Sarah said, "just remember, the Bible tells us that the rain falls on those who live right as well as those who don't. We don't know anything about this girl and her family."

"You're right, Sarah," Holly said, contrite. "I just wish the rain would fall on us a little more right now. We could really use it."

Sarah steered her car into the driveway of Bethany's house, put it in park, and then gave both of the girls a soft smile of understanding.

"I understand where you two are coming from—I really do. But I want you to think about this: Sometimes when the rain falls, it isn't always a good thing. Sometimes it can be the beginning of a pretty bad storm. Let's be patient. The money for our trip will come. We are lucky we have God with us through the good times—as well as the bad."

Bethany suddenly felt a chill go up her back. She remembered her dream ... and then remembered the look of sadness on the girl's face as she glanced up through the window of that limousine.

Whatever gave her that sad look, money wasn't curing it. Bethany prayed for the girl and then she wondered if the girl knew God.

Bethany felt herself being drawn back into another memory: the morning of the shark attack when she'd lost her arm ... She tried to imagine what it would've been like if *she* hadn't known God when it happened.

I don't know that girl, God, Bethany silently prayed. *But you do, and I think she could use your help right now.* Bethany thought about what Sarah had said, then quickly added. *Me too; I have a feeling there's still a lot I gotta learn ...*

"It says here that we should come across a small stream just before we get to the parking lot for the trail," Andrea said only seconds before the rental car suddenly dipped into a six-inch stream running over the road. She bit her lip to keep from laughing.

"Great timing!" Her mom laughed, turning into the parking area. Andrea exhaled, relieved that her mom had taken it so well. Dead ahead of them was the ocean, and to the left was a steep velvet-green cliff that soared straight up, hundreds of feet into the air. Hikers were everywhere with backpacks and walking sticks. One group even packed a baby in a baby carrier.

"Want to stretch a little before we take off?" Andrea's mom asked.

"Sure. Should we bring the sunscreen with us?" said Andrea.

"A good thing you remembered that. We would've been burned to a crisp!"

Andrea beamed at the compliment. She still couldn't believe that they were going hiking together—that her mom had actually turned off her cell phone, wished her dad and brother well fishing, and then tore out of their vacation home like a woman on a mission. Andrea snuck a glance at her mom as they did leg squats and stretches on the beach.

They had been on vacations before—stayed in other beautiful places with awesome views—but those had been *working vacations*, as her parents liked to say. Which basically meant she and her brother, Mark, were left to explore with assistants or tour guides instead of their parents. This time was different, but it felt shaky too. Like her Uncle Mike's death had shaken them awake, but they weren't sure where to go from there.

"Okay! Let's do it!" Her mom said, sliding her backpack on.

Andrea quickly shrugged into her small pack as well and followed her mom to the entrance of the trail. Then she spotted the well-worn path that shot upward at a forty-five degree angle, and she stopped dead in her tracks.

"Are you sure I can do this?"

Her mom turned around and gave her an encouraging smile. "You're my daughter, aren't you? Of course you can do this!"

Andrea shrugged shyly. "I mean, you and dad might have hiked Mount Kilimanjaro when you were young, but the highest thing I've climbed lately is the bleachers at school."

"Kilimanjaro was *fifteen* years ago," her mom said. "But, if it'll make you feel any better, I think I took the stairs at work one day last week."

They both laughed and were evidently so pleased at the sound of their laughter— together—that neither of them noticed the small well-worn sign at the entrance of the trailhead that read "Danger! Do not leave trail. Steep cliffs, crumbling rock."

three

"Come on, Holly! It's not dangerous!"

"I looked like a maniac when I got home from the run this morning. I never look that crazy after surfing," Holly said on the other end of the phone. Bethany couldn't help smiling. "And it's uphill half the way!"

"And downhill the other half," Bethany coaxed as she sorted through her CDs. "Come on, it'll be fun *and* a good workout!"

"Okay, okay."

"Oh, and bring some shoes you can actually run in. Junky ones if you have them 'cause of the mud." Bethany winced and then rushed on, hoping Holly would miss the part about the mud. "We'll go early in the morning, and I'll ask my mom to bring our boards and stuff when she comes to pick us up. That way we can surf after the run."

"How is she going to know what time to get us? Cell phones don't work out that far," said Holly.

"Not on the trail, but they do at the end of the road. My mom used to train out there."

"Well, just so you know, I'm not sure I want to run all the way to the falls."

"Why not?" asked Bethany.

Holly dropped her voice to a whisper. "I heard there are creepy people who hang out back there."

Bethany smiled to herself. "Nah, just Kauai bares," she whispered back mischievously.

"Bears?" Holly asked, her voice suddenly a little panicky. "We have bears on Kauai? We don't even have snakes, how could we have bears?"

"I'm surprised you haven't seen them before," Bethany said, all serious. "They travel in pairs most of the time. Oh, and every once in a while you'll see them dressed in hats and shoes … but that's about it."

"You've lost me … Wait! Are you talking about those crazies that get out in the back country and take off all of their clothes?"

"Yep! Kauai bares … get it?" Bethany laughed. "B-A-R-E-S!"

Holly laughed. "I like trustafarians better."

"Me too," Bethany giggled. "They wear clothes."

After they set a time to meet, Bethany flipped her phone closed and leaned back against the pillows on her bed. She should've been tired after all she had done today, but she was way too excited to be tired. Besides, it wasn't dinnertime yet.

She scrambled off the bed and dragged her daypack and hiking gear out of her closet. Not only was she looking forward to running the Hanakapiai Trail in the morning, but she was even more excited about the surf-a-thon—and the idea had come when her friend Liam popped into her head.

If there was anyone who knew how to raise funds for a good cause, it was Liam. The surf contest he'd held in California for handicapped kids was not only successful, it was also a blast to participate in.

Bethany smiled as she packed. How wild it was that God had put Liam in her path—and how Liam had been inspired to do something for handicapped kids after they met. And now Liam was inspiring her to do something for others too. And he didn't even know it! She'd definitely have to write and tell him about everything—after she got back from her run with Holly to the falls. With Holly along, she was sure there would be more to report back to Liam.

Bethany's smile faltered for a moment as the memory of the girl from the limousine popped into her head again. Bethany wondered how her hike to the falls was going. She shook her head, not really understanding why someone she didn't even know would be on her mind—especially someone who seemed to have everything.

Still, the memory of her sad face lingered.

Long way down, Andrea thought as she and her mom stopped for a breather. They had been concentrating so hard on making it over the slippery boulders and around the mud puddles that they hadn't realized they had climbed hundreds of feet. Until they stopped to view the scene below.

It was a breathtaking view. The massive Na Pali cliffs were tipped in mist as they snaked along the coastline. They were so beautiful and immense, they almost didn't seem real.

"I heard *Jurassic Park* was filmed here," Andrea said, her voice soft with awe, and her mom nodded.

"I can see why," said her mom. "It almost looks prehistoric."

Andrea bit the inside of her lip, thinking as she took it all in: the bowl of blue sky above them; the cliffs, bigger than anything she had ever seen; the trees; even the ocean below that spread out as far as the eye could see. *It was just too beautiful to be an accident. Why haven't I ever thought of that before? Why did it take Uncle Mike's death for me to wonder about life?*

She knew a lot of kids thought she had it made, but the truth was she felt like there was something *missing* inside her most of the time. She had so many questions—questions she didn't even know how to ask—or maybe was afraid to ask ...

Andrea glanced over at her mom who was studying the sky, and she wondered if her mom was thinking about her uncle Mike. Did her mother wonder what happened when people die or if there really was a heaven or a God? She took a deep breath and plunged in before she could think of being scared again.

"Mom … do you ever wonder if there is a God?"

Her mom gave her a quick look of surprise, then turned back to look at the sky. "I guess it's kind of hard not to wonder when you see something like this," she answered slowly, then frowned. "I know you have a lot of questions about Uncle Mike. We all do. But your dad and I have always prided ourselves in being thinkers—thinking for ourselves, believing in what we could make out of our lives. It just doesn't seem rational to depend on something or someone you're not even sure exists."

Andrea felt like a balloon that had been deflated. She'd really hoped her mom might say something to help her with the "something's missing" feeling.

"Time to roll out, kiddo. I want to get back to the boys by dinner!"

Andrea was caught off guard as her mom suddenly hooked her arm in hers as they continued on the trail. It felt good, though, so she wasn't about to mess it up with any more questions.

As they continued on, the mud became something they could no longer dodge, and their legs and shoes were heavy with the goo.

"I didn't expect it to be this wet," her mom said suddenly. "It was so nice when we started out. How did it get chilly so quickly?"

The trail turned slippery, making their way up even more difficult. Andrea suddenly felt uneasy.

"Do you think we should turn back?"

"Let's keep going," her mom said between breaths as they struggled on up the steep, slippery trail. "It can't be that much farther."

A turn in the footpath, and the falls came into view—still several miles away but close enough to spur the hikers on.

The last two miles turned out to be almost treacherous; each time the trail switched over the stream, crossing became harder. The force of the water almost knocked them over. A light rain began to dribble down through the canopy of trees and onto the hikers. Fear coursed through Andrea with almost as much force as the stream. But she pushed ahead, unwilling to admit her fears to her mother.

Finally, they heard the deep steady roar of water. As they stepped into a clearing, they saw the cascading white water, powerfully hurling down hundreds of feet of cliff.

They smiled at each other, and for the next twenty minutes under a thick umbrella of trees, everything seemed okay again. They ate a late lunch that Andrea's mom had packed. Andrea even waded into the shallow side of the large pond beneath the falls for her mom to snap some photos—and then they decided to head back.

Easier said than done, Andrea thought, trudging through the rain until they came to the edge of the stream that ran across the trail. The same stream that they had crossed to get to the falls was now a lot deeper.

"We need to hurry," her mom said suddenly, and Andrea glanced over. Her mom trudged on through the water, giving her no further explanation. She didn't need to, Andrea thought, as she noticed the water level rising with each stream they crossed.

The last stream they hit had become a raging torrent of water. Andrea saw the beads of sweat on her mom's brow, and she knew they were in trouble.

"Mom?"

She followed her mom's gaze, knowing she was looking for another way across for them — and then felt a massive chill run over her as her mom stopped and studied a narrow little trail that seemed to hang over the side of the cliff.

Oh, no way! Andrea thought just as her mom said, "Let's try that trail."

The narrow little goat trail did seem the way out at first, but after the second hair-pin turn, they were forced to drop down on all fours, and shortly after that, the trail hit a dead end. They both glanced behind them; the way back looked impossible to manage. The trail was too narrow to turn around on, and neither of them felt comfortable going backward.

Andrea followed her mom's eyes as she studied what looked like another trail high above them, and she felt whatever strength she had left whoosh out of her.

"Andrea, you stay put. I'm going to see if there's a way out up there. If there is, then I'll help you get up to it too."

Andrea merely nodded, too cold and scared to argue. Instead, she plastered herself to the face of the cliff as her mom began to climb.

Maybe fifteen or twenty minutes later, she heard a dribble of rock skittering down the face of the cliff and looked up to see her mom on a ledge that jutted out above her. It was getting dark—harder to see—but she was sure that her mom looked like she had been crying.

"Andrea, it's going to take me awhile to get out of this." Her mom said this with such a forced calmness to her voice that it scared Andrea even more. "Just hang on."

"All right," Andrea called out and then pressed back against the cliff. *It's not all right, though. It's not all right at all*, Andrea thought as tears began to course down her cheeks. She watched the sun slowly dip down, and she watched the green of the trees and brush turn a darker shade of green as the mist thickened around them.

Still too beautiful to be an accident, she thought as exhaustion began to take over. *God, if you are up there, well, we could sure use your help.*

four

"*Nice* shoes!" said Holly.

"Hey, these shoes have seen a lot of hikes," Bethany said, grinning over at Holly as they scrambled out of the van at the entrance to Hanakapiai Trail. "And look—Velcro fasteners!"

"How seventies of you." Holly grinned back, feeling perky with her hair back to normal. "Did that dragged-behind-the-van look come with the shoes, or did you do that after you bought them?"

Bethany laughed out loud. "I'm doubling the pace on you for that, Holly! You try to tie shoes with one hand sometime."

"No thanks! I'm having a hard enough time keeping up with your training sessions as it is!"

They both laughed and then looked upwards as a helicopter flew overhead.

"Awful early for sightseeing," Bethany noted.

"Be careful girls, and give me a call when you want to get picked up," Bethany's mom called from the van as she pulled away. "Oh, and I heard it's been raining up in the mountains, so keep an eye out for flooding."

Holly turned and looked up at the mountains as Bethany's mom drove away. "Flooding? Why do I listen to you?"

"Because without me your life would be boring," Bethany said with a grin. "Okay, are you ready?"

"Yeah—at least I hope I am!"

They started out in a light jog. In the first few hundred yards of the steep trail they easily passed out-of-shape hikers who hadn't gotten more than a few dozen yards before stopping to catch their breath.

Bethany and Holly grinned at each other, feeling a little full of themselves. They were blowing by everyone!

As they passed the vista, the trail began to hug the edge of the cliff, zigzagging back and forth without steps, railings, or safety bars, and they both eased back on their pace—but not by much. Recent rain had created small, unavoidable puddles and they splashed through them, trying to hit the water hard enough to get each other wet.

Then the trail slipped around the side of the cliff again and Bethany felt her right shoe hit a patch of mud which sent her skidding and sliding.

Bethany flailed awkwardly, trying to regain her footing. She was suddenly hit with the weirdest sensation—a mini flashback of her dream of falling backwards. She stumbled to the left, then caught herself just in time and glanced over at Holly shakily. For the first time in a long while, she didn't feel so sure of her abilities.

"I had no idea it was going to be this muddy!" Bethany said when she found her voice again. "Let's take it easy until the trail gets better."

"Good idea," Holly said quietly as her eyes scanned the empty trail ahead worriedly. "Last thing we need is to get hurt with no one else around to help."

"Andrea!"

The voice sounded muffled at first ... far away. Andrea frowned. She was too tired to try to figure out where the voice was coming from. Too tired to care.

She felt her stomach growl. When she did get up she was going straight for the huge fruit basket she'd spotted on the table in the entryway, maybe take a dip in the pool out back. That ought to wake her up.

"Andrea!!!" the voice persisted, and Andrea sat up groggily—then caught herself before she fell off the tiny ledge. *Oh ... my ... God!* She wasn't at home in bed. She was still trapped on the side of a cliff!

"Andrea!" her mom's terror-stricken voice called from above, and she carefully craned her neck and looked up. Her mom's face looked pale and ... terrified.

"Mom, I'm okay! I just feel asleep," she called out and then swallowed painfully. Her water bottle was almost empty; she took a small sip and swished it around in her mouth before swallowing it.

"Did you try your cell phone again?" she called up to her mom.

"Still no signal on the cell," her mom answered after a moment. "But I heard a helicopter earlier, honey. I bet someone is going to find us any minute now!"

Andrea licked her cracked lips as her body began to shiver uncontrollably. She gazed out across the vast 5,000-foot-high ribbon of emerald cliffs that plunged almost straight down to the ocean.

What was beautiful yesterday was overwhelming now. Overwhelming and ugly. She squinted hard into the dawning light but could see nothing but trees and large bushes. A lot of them. It seemed so big—too big. How could anyone find her or her mom in the middle of all this?

Like finding a needle in a haystack. That was a crazy thing to hope for, she thought dully. Who ever thought that one up? Andrea suddenly remembered her prayer from the night before, and her eyes welled up with tears.

God, if you are there, please send help! Andrea's mind screamed. Her plea was met with an eerie silence as her eyes desperately searched the vast wilderness for any sign of a hiker. Even the birds were silent.

God finding her here felt a lot like finding a needle in a haystack. She had never talked to God before. She wondered if she was saying the right words. One of her friends had taken her to church before. She knew that her friend talked to God, actually felt love for God. Andrea frowned. Why would God listen to her? Thinking God could hear her was probably a crazy thing to hope for.

"Look what I found!"

Holly held the shell out for Bethany to see as they squatted in the sand by the stream. They had found the little slip of sand and stream after a precarious climb over some massive rocks and boulders. They decided to take a short break by hunting for the shells that were known to be harvested along this stretch.

Bethany felt a twinge of good-natured envy. It was a sunset shell—better than any she had in her collection at home.

"Oh my gosh! Look at the size of that shell! You totally scored!" Bethany threw her hand up in defeat, and Holly laughed delightedly. It wasn't every day that she got one up on Bethany, and they both knew it.

The truth was, Bethany was glad for the momentary distraction. Nearly falling like she did had shaken her up more than she cared to admit. For some reason, it had made her feel helpless—like she had felt right after the shark attack and even in that crazy dream. She didn't like that feeling. Not one bit.

Bethany glanced toward the trail that led to the falls and felt a little bit of the fighter in her rise up. She needed to get over this nagging fear and press on—just as she had done so many times while surfing or training.

Do something big, she thought.

"Let's go to the falls!" Bethany said suddenly.

"What? Two more miles—are you nuts?" Holly exclaimed as she shoved the shell in her pocket. "Huh-uh. I'm not doing it." She watched Bethany knock the mud from her shoes for a moment, frowned, and then followed suit.

"I must be crazy," she grumbled, and Bethany chuckled.

"Maybe," Bethany said as she started over the rocks and boulders and then turned to look over her shoulder. "But it's a *good* kind of crazy!"

High on her perch, Andrea peered into the valley and watched for hikers. When she first woke up, she had pretty much given up. But as the day wore on, she and her mom had caught glimpses of several hikers, appearing and disappearing as they followed along the trail below. It had been her first ray of hope since the night before.

Getting their attention had been another thing altogether ...

They had screamed their guts out, but it appeared that the echo of their voices had been drained away by the wind. The hikers moved on, oblivious to their predicament.

"They can't hear us!" Andrea yelled up frantically to her mom.

"We're going to have to shout louder!"

It was another twenty minutes before they heard the thump of a helicopter, and their hope rose again—only to be dashed as they watched the whir of blades fade off into the distance.

When she heard her mom curse above her, she felt what little hope she had begin to seep out of her, and she began to cry.

Along with the release of tears, Andrea felt a strong sense of peace came over her. She stopped thinking about the danger and noticed the warm sun and gentle wind. They felt comforting to her. She heard a strong inner voice saying *Don't lose hope!* It was such a strong feeling, that she actually felt a surge of hope and determination. For the first time since they were stranded, she felt like she could think clearly.

"You have got to think of some way to attract attention," her mom called down with more than a tinge of desperation in her voice. "Nobody can see me, but they can probably see you from that spot. Keep watching for people hiking on the trail and try to find some way to get their attention."

"I'm working on something right now!" Andrea called up to her.

Actually, she had been working on the plan since she heard the voice that whispered in her heart. For the last hour she had been slowly digging rocks and hard clumps of dirt out of the face of the cliff with one of her shoes. It seemed crazy, she thought, staring with a strange kind of satisfaction at the small pile next to her. But it seemed right too. Like the inner voice that had whispered to her, urging her to keep going and not to give up. Something about it just felt right.

Bethany felt her determination grow as they skirted around the thin valley trail. She hopped over Hanakapiai Stream each time it cut across the trail. The farther they climbed, the more she made an effort to squash the feeling of helplessness that had tried to overtake her.

"I'm a believer, help me believe," Holly suddenly sang at the top of her lungs, shocking Bethany from her thoughts. It was the Switchfoot song they'd been singing in the van after church ealier this week. Not really knowing why, Bethany felt compelled to join in:

"And I gave it all away and lost who I am, I threw it all away with everything to gain, and I'm taking the leap ..." They both laughed and leaped over the stream.

Bethany glanced back just in time to see Holly pick up a rock and heave it into the water with enough force to splash the back of her legs.

"Hey!"

Before Bethany had time to scramble for a rock of her own, several rocks hit the water. Holly, empty-handed, gave Bethany a stunned look just as another torrent of rocks hit the water.

"Rock slide!" Holly yelled, and they both retreated away from the wall of the canyon. More rocks followed, some bouncing down the cliff and others hitting the stream. They both lifted their eyes to the top of the cliff ... and that's when they saw her. Or a fuzzy version of her. Their eyes locked on the teenager far above them as they stepped from their hiding place, and she quickly realized they saw her too. She began to wave frantically.

"What's wrong?" Bethany called up to her.

"We're stuck. We can't get down!" she cried out.

Bethany turned to Holly. "Let's go," was all she said—all she had to say—and the two of them began to carefully work their way up the cliff side.

Bethany soon realized that the muddy slide at the beginning of the trail was nothing compared to the steep path that led to the girl's position—*too steep to traverse without being able to use* both *hands and feet*, the mean voice of fear said as it slid through her. After going fifteen feet from the valley floor, she stopped and turned to Holly, who was following close behind.

"I'm not sure I can do this climb—not without two arms to hold onto rocks and things. What do you think?"

"I think we should tell her we'll go get help," Holly suggested.

They squinted back up to where the girl was, and just as they did, they were horrified to see her suddenly lose her footing and begin to tumble and slide down the side of the cliff.

A woman's voice came out of nowhere, echoing over them in a shriek of terror.

"No time for that, *now!*" Bethany exclaimed as she quickly scrambled in the direction of the girl's fall.

five

If there was ever a time when Bethany felt that she might have made a wrong decision, she figured it was the moment she threw all caution to the wind and began her climb up the side of the cliff to the spot where the girl was now clinging to an exposed root she had latched onto on her way down.

The muscles in her right arm were screaming from overexertion as she tried to grab onto rocks and stumps that would help pull her up. She knew Holly was coaching her along from the valley below, but all she could hear for the moment were her own ragged gasps.

Just a little farther.

Bethany suddenly felt her right foot slip. She started to slide down, but she grabbed onto a clump of brush and leaned into it, trying to ease the strain on her arm. *I'm not going to make it,* she thought as fear mixed in with her sweat and slid like a cold chill down her back. She looked up and saw the girl's face swimming out of focus just a short distance above her, and she wished she had the strength to tell the girl that she was sorry.

Please, God! I can't do this! she thought, feeling herself begin to fall backward—just like her dream, but it wasn't a dream this time. This was for real.

"Bethany!" Holly yelled.

Bethany's arm pinwheeled like crazy as she tried to get her balance back. She felt nauseous and light-headed, like she was going to black out.

I'm done for ...

"You can do it!" the girl suddenly called out, tears running down her face as she held onto the root for dear life. "I *prayed* that God would send help. I don't know that much about God, but I don't think he'd let you fail ... if he sent you."

"God, please help me!" Bethany gasped. Bethany bent her knees and leaned forward. Suddenly she wasn't falling anymore. She felt her grip strengthen on a wad of branches.

"When we are weak, he is strong," Holly yelled from below. "Remember what Sarah told us! God will give you strength when you need it!"

Bethany took a deep, ragged breath and reached up. She felt the rocky ledge scrape against the bottom of her hand and she gasped. Not out of pain ... but surprise.

It was just like her dream! She grabbed ahold of the ledge with one hand, and as she did, she remembered the words, "I AM the rock!"

God is my shelter from the storm. He is the rock that gives me refuge from the waves. He is my strength. Why didn't I understand that before?!

Bethany felt tears spring to her eyes as she pulled herself another foot closer to the girl. "Please help me," she prayed out loud. "I can't do this without you!"

Amazingly, she felt a surge of energy and confidence, and she was able to keep going.

A few more feet and Bethany had finally drawn close enough to see the girl's face. She was battered and bruised, but still pretty enough to recognize. It was the same girl from the limousine! Bethany dug her feet into the rocky hillside, finally finding a foothold on a ledge that was strong enough to hold the weight of both of them. She leaned into the girl so she could slowly slide down into position to stand with Bethany on the ledge.

Standing together for the first time, they looked at each other and smiled. Then the girl started to cry, and soon Bethany was crying too.

Through her tears, Bethany barely heard Holly yelling up to the woman above them that she was going for help. Bethany wanted to say something to Holly, but all she could do for the moment was hang on to the girl and thank God over and over for what he had done.

"My name is Andrea," the girl said when she was finally able to speak. "And *you* are the answer to my very first prayer."

"Wow," Bethany said softly, trying to swallow past the lump in her throat. "Most people just call me Bethany."

There was a short pause, then Bethany asked, "So, where are you from?"

"Colorado."

"Huh. How did you end up getting stuck all the way out here?"

God has a sense of humor, Holly thought as she ran back down the steep, winding trail. *He really has a sense of humor!* Not only was Bethany the last person that should be sent scrambling up the side of a cliff, but she, Holly Silva, was the *very* last person that should be sent on a downhill death run!

"Please let me make it. Please let them be all right," Holly prayed over and over in beat with her run as she continued to wind her way down the mountain, running as fast as her legs would carry her.

The path tilted even steeper and Holly pushed herself harder. Her lungs were burning, but she ignored the pain and continued to run.

The path turned muddy again. For a moment it twisted up and then pitched down again, going around a sharp corner. Holly would have preferred to lie down somewhere and pass out from fear and exhaustion. Instead, she kept going.

"Please let me make it. Please let them be all right ..."

Hitting a particularly slick spot at full stride, Holly suddenly felt the traction in both shoes give way, and before she knew what had happened, she was sliding off of the trail. Then her backside smashed up against a huge boulder, stopping her fall, but not the destruction of the cell phone in her back pocket.

She got up, even more determined than before, and began to run again, changing her prayer only slightly: "Please let me make it. Please let them be all right. Please send someone with a cell phone!"

The steep downhill drop turned into a city of boulders. Holly surprised herself and bounded over the boulders like a billy goat. She ran out over a tangle of roots and past the trailhead sign. Finally! She was at the bottom, sore and out of breath.

Gasping for air, she glanced around, trying to find someone with a cell phone.

Suddenly she noticed a couple coming from the parking lot. They were loaded down with huge and very expensive-looking backpacks. The man had thick, dark dreadlocks. He was wearing beads around his neck and a Grateful Dead T-shirt. The woman with him wore loose peasant clothes and had small tattoos tracked around her wrist and upper arm.

Trustafarians! God, you really outdid yourself this time! This is just who I needed!

"Excuse me, you wouldn't have a cell phone I could borrow?" Holly asked as she tried to rub the mud and grime off of her face. "It's an emergency."

It wasn't long before Bethany and Andrea heard the heavy thwack of the first helicopter as it moved slowly around the ridge. The bright red helicopter suddenly popped into view. The words County Rescue Helicopter were emblazoned on its side.

"Woohoo!" Bethany yelled, and Andrea laughed a tired kind of laugh, leaning against the cliff and hugging Bethany tightly as a blast of wind from the helicopter blew over them. They watched the pilot maneuver into position and then lower the first rescue person to the area where Andrea's mom was.

Soon her mom was swinging out into the air with her rescuer, and then they were both sucked upwards towards the chopper.

The next rescue was a little trickier. Because of the girls' position against the cliff, the rescuers had to drop into the valley and climb up, much like Bethany had done—except they each had mountain-climbing gear.

And two arms.

That detail wasn't lost on them as the first rescuer finally reached Bethany and Andrea's small perch.

"How in the world did *you* make it up here?" he asked in wide-eyed amazement. Bethany looked at Andrea and smiled, then turned back to the rescuer.

"God," she answered simply. The man smiled and shook his head as he quickly strapped her in with him. Then the second rescuer arrived, and the question was asked again as he strapped Andrea in with him.

"A whole lot of prayer," Andrea added.

"Stick to surfing next time, okay?" the second man, a Hawaiian, said with a grin. Bethany looked at her rescuer again and then recognized him as a regular in one of the local surf spots.

"No problem! Scout's honor and all that!" she said emphatically.

Her rescuer gave the chopper above them the "thumbs-up" sign, and suddenly they were wrenched out from the face of the cliff and immediately swung out over the precipice.

By the time Bethany mustered the courage to look down again, Andrea and her rescuer looked like ants under the other helicopter. She gazed past them, then straight down to see ocean waves crashing against the vertical face of Na Pali a thousand feet below her. The view nearly took her breath away—would've taken her breath away if it weren't for the two scruffy, mud-caked shoes dangling in her line of vision.

I gotta get some new shoes, Bethany thought with a tired sigh.

Andrea had never seen her dad or her brother look so happy as they did when she and her mom stepped out of the helicopter. He and Mark ran toward them at breakneck speed.

"What were you trying to do, give me a heart attack?" Mark said breathlessly as he hugged his sister tightly. He turned away to swipe his tears with the back of his hand. Andrea's tears flowed freely as she turned to hug her dad.

"Oh, thank God!" Her dad exclaimed, as he opened his arms to include them all in a bear hug.

"That's exactly who we should thank, Dad," Andrea said tiredly. "I prayed that God would help us get down safely from there," she said as they all headed toward the rental car.

"I guess we were both doing quite a bit of praying up there, Darryl," Andrea's mom admitted, shocking them all into momentary silence. She bit her lip as she looked at her family, hesitated, and then plunged ahead. "I made a deal with God up there, a promise that I hope you all will help me keep."

Andrea's dad drew back to look at her mom, a look of puzzlement on his face.

"Can you do that? Can you make a deal with God?"

Her mom laughed—a tired kind of laugh, but it sounded so good to Andrea.

"Don't look at me like that! I'm not going to become a nun or run off and join some commune."

She took a deep breath. "I had a lot of time to think up there. I couldn't help thinking about Mike, thinking how fortunate I am to have you, Andrea, and Mark … and how quickly that could all go away.

"I promised God that if he got us off that cliff safely, I would start going to church—to find out more about him. And I was hoping you and the kids would go with me."

"I'm so there," Andrea said as she jumped in the car. Her brother took his turn at looking puzzled. She didn't care. Something good was happening, and she didn't want to lose it.

"Dad, you and Mark should have seen it! We had been out on that cliff all night. We were so tired and feeling hopeless. Nobody could hear us or see us, and I was praying like crazy. And all of a sudden I heard these girls singing—like angels, but singing Christian rock. But that's how I found them—how they found me! Then the one girl saw me slipping and started climbing to help me. She only had one arm! I was so scared for her, but then she started asking God to help her. I knew she was the answer to *my* prayer!"

Andrea glanced at her brother who was listening intently, his iPod still in his hands.

"Did you get their names?" Her dad asked suddenly. When he turned to look at her, she was surprised to see tears in his eyes. "I would really like to thank the both of them."

"The girl with one arm is named Bethany," Andrea said and then frowned, trying to remember. "I think she called the other girl Holly."

"Well, it would be nice if we could find them before we leave," her dad said casually, but his eyes said something more. He looked like a man on a mission.

six

Morning at the Hamilton household was in full
swing by the time Bethany staggered stiffly out
of her bedroom and headed into the kitchen.
She was starting to feel the aftereffects of the day
before. The cuts had stopped bleeding, but she
knew from the dull pain on her upper leg that she
would have a nasty bruise to deal with. Her dog,
Ginger, appeared, her tail wagging like crazy as
she nudged Bethany to be petted.

"I am soooooo sore." Bethany winced and then
caught her brothers smirking at each other across
the kitchen table. She narrowed her eyes at them.
Definitely no sympathy from the peanut gallery.

"Hey, Bethany, I'm thinking about taking a hike
into Hanakapiai this morning. Wanna come?" Noah
asked, trying to sound innocent.

"We even found some shoes for you to wear."
Tim grinned and held up her old battered shoes—
the same shoes she'd dumped in the trash as soon
as she'd made it home the night before—between

two fingers and waved them in the air. Bethany grimaced.

"I don't care if I *never* take that hike again," she declared, trying not to laugh at Tim as he wiggled his eyebrows at her. "I hiked it enough in one day to last the rest of my life!"

"Dad, you should've seen how Bethany and Holly fell asleep in the van last night," Tim said with a grin. "Bethany's got her muddy face pressed against the window—out like a light—and Holly's in the backseat, leaning back with her mouth wide open. I would've given my right arm to have had my camera with me!"

"Very funny, Tim!"

"Well, your mom and I are really proud of what you did," her dad said, coming up behind her. Bethany ducked her head shyly.

"Besides," her dad said with a smile, "knowing you, within a week or so you'll have forgotten all about it and be raring to go again."

"No way!" Bethany said and then laughed. "Well, I'm *pretty* sure it's 'no way.' Swimming there might not be too bad."

Her dad groaned.

"She's just like you, Tom," her mom said as she flipped the eggs over in the pan. "Don't forget that everyone called you Dolphin Man because you would swim like a crazy person at all the beaches around the island."

Tom laughed, and for one strange moment Bethany saw herself in the way he laughed. "I tell you what, Bethany, if you decide to take your surfboard to Hanakapiai, I'll go with you."

"Cool!"

"And I'll bring the boat to rescue you two nut cases ... and anybody else Bethany talks into that crazy scheme," Noah added.

"That would be ... Holly," Bethany said, and they all laughed.

"You and Holly could almost be twins today," Sarah said with a warm smile as Bethany eased herself out of the van and slowly walked alongside the youth director.

"Twins of pain," Bethany said with a smile of her own as she glanced around.

The parking lot at Pine Trees Beach was already jammed with the regulars for the day. Their empty racks and wax-stained roofs glistened in the sun. *Great day to surf ... if I wasn't so sore.* Bethany spotted Holly hunched down in a chair by the table Sarah had set up at the far end of the crescent-shaped lot. Bethany waved to her. Holly waved back, along with the rest of gang from the Hanalei Girls Surf Team.

"So, what's our plan of attack?" Bethany asked as they headed for the table.

"Filling up these pledge forms for the surf-a-thon," Sarah said, handing her a sheet from the stack she carried. "We need to get as many people as we can to make pledges." Sarah smiled. "You and Holly get to park yourselves at the table since you've been voted Heroes for the Day."

Bethany blushed. "I wouldn't exactly call us heroes. It was more like we were at the right place and the right time for God to use us." She glanced over at Sarah. "You were right, by the way: When we are weak, he *is* strong. There is just no way I could've made that climb without God's help." She shook her head. "And then I got there and not only found out that it was the same girl we saw in the limo, but she told me she had prayed—first time in her whole life—and I was her answer!"

"Yeah," Sarah nodded thoughtfully, tears welling up in her eyes. "It's always been my experience that when God shows up like that, it's to do a work that will affect not just one life, but a *lot* of lives."

"That's so awesome."

"Little old lady number two has arrived!" Monica announced as Bethany slowly limped up to the table. She rolled her eyes at Monica as Malia and Jenna gave her a quick hug, and then she slid into the chair next to Holly.

"Kinda sore today?" Bethany asked, and Holly gave her an incredulous look.

"*Kinda?* I can barely move! Not to mention I couldn't get to sleep—even after all my relatives left. I just kept thinking that God has a great sense of humor; the 'trustafarians' being the ones who loaned me a cell phone, and the 'celebutante' being the girl stranded on the cliff!"

Bethany laughed.

"What's a celebutante?" Jenna asked curiously.

"Oh, that's the new name Holly made up for Monica," Bethany teased, winking at Jenna and Malia.

"Celebutante?" Monica flipped her hair as she glanced at each of their grinning faces. "What's that supposed to mean?"

The girls laughed — even Monica *after* she caught on that Bethany was teasing her — and then quickly got down to business.

"Okay," Bethany said, shuffling through their pledge sheets. "We gotta get some people to sign up quickly if we're going to make this surf-a-thon a success."

"Mexico is going to be awesome!" Malia said excitedly.

"I know," Bethany said. "I've been wanting to do something like this *forever*."

"Can you believe we're going to build houses for people?" Holly shook her head.

"Can you believe anyone would want to live in a house a bunch of high school kids built?" Jenna said. "Talk about some brave people!"

"Get much training building houses in Arizona?" Monica said, glancing at Jenna.

"About as much as you have in Hawaii," Jenna retorted, and the girls laughed.

"Okay, okay, I give!" Monica declared. "You guys know I really want to do this too," she added, looking around their little group. "I'm just hoping and praying we can make enough with all of this fundraising to get us there!"

"You never know how God's going to work it all out," Bethany said, giving Holly a wink. "But that's the fun part."

"Fun?"

"Yeah," Holly said as a slow grin spread across her face. "You gotta think of it kind of like a mystery—and God is the one who leaves us clues along the way."

"Sometimes, you don't even realize they're clues until the end of the mystery," Bethany added and then turned and gazed towards the ocean.

She didn't know exactly how they were going to get that money. She was pretty good at imagining stuff, and even she couldn't imagine a way! But then, after everything that had happened, she also knew with all of her heart that if she did her part, God would work it out for the best.

When I am weak, you are shown strong through me, she thought.

"How old do you think they were, Susan?" said Andrea's dad.

"I don't know ... close to Andrea's age."

"We don't have much to go on."

"I feel badly that we didn't get their full names, Darryl. Everything just happened so quickly after the rescue," Andrea's mom said as the family rode in the back of the limo around the island. Andrea watched her dad pat her mom's arm affectionately, and she marveled at how much things had changed in such a short period of time.

"We have so much to be grateful for," he'd said over breakfast. "So much!"

Breakfast that morning had been kind of like Thanksgiving, with the way her dad and brother had loaded the table down with huge bowls of tropical fruit, french toast, eggs, and tall glasses of orange juice. Her stomach had sure been thankful, she thought, as she smiled to herself.

"Andrea and I prayed we'd find them this morning," her mom said, sending a smile Andrea's way. "We're just going to have to have faith that we will."

Andrea's dad looked almost mystified as he stared back at her mom—like he wasn't sure just yet how to react to this new attitude from his wife.

Andrea understood the look. The praying and the talk about faith were so new to all of them—it was almost like learning another language. But it felt good and ... so right! She glanced over at Mark, who looked content to see his family getting along so well.

"Bethany is the girl I told you about with one arm," Andrea supplied. "I know what she looks like for sure, but I barely saw the other girl." Andrea frowned, trying to pull something from her memory, but she came up empty.

"Okay, we got their first names and ... somewhat of a description," her dad said, chewing thoughtfully on his lip. "Now we have to find them ... somewhere on this island."

Like finding a needle in a haystack, Andrea thought worriedly and then suddenly caught herself in mid-thought, remembering how God had proved her wrong the last time she had that thought. She smiled. *God seemed to be real good at finding needles in haystacks.*

"You say that one of the girls was a surfer?" the driver asked suddenly as he gazed at Andrea in the rearview mirror.

"I remember the rescuer telling her to stick to surfing," Andrea said slowly, and the Hawaiian bobbed his head.

"We'll go to the north side," he said, and then smiled at the family's collective look of confusion. "Best surf spots around."

Sarah glanced through the pledge sheets as Bethany, Holly, and several others hovered around her table. She kept a serious face, pretending to go over the paperwork a little longer while the teens held their breath.

"How did we do?" Bethany asked, unable to bear the suspense any longer.

"Not too bad," Sarah answered with a cheerful smile. "Remember, every little bit gets us that much closer!"

Bethany nearly groaned out loud as she watched Sarah pick her pen up and tap it against the table, thinking. *Every little bit gets us that much closer* meant that they were still way off of their goal.

Holly nudged her, breaking into her thoughts. "Remember, we never know how God will work it out!" she said with a wink.

Bethany smiled and shook her head. Holly was right, of course. It was just hard teaching herself to think a new way. And patience had always been a tough one for her.

"All right, let's get this stuff put away," Sarah said, pushing away from the table. "Bethany, can you take the sign down across the street?"

"I'm on it," Bethany said, taking off in a slow jog towards the sign. Just then her brother Tim pulled in to pick her up.

"Better hurry up," Tim called out the window. "You too, Holly, unless you both are in the mood for another hike!"

Andrea didn't want to give up the search for Bethany and Holly, but they were quickly running out of options. They had been to nearly every surf spot the driver knew of, and there was still no sign of the two girls. She pressed her forehead against the window and watched the scenery go by.

"One more surf spot coming up," the driver announced. "You want me to stop?"

"I don't know," Andrea's mom said softly, still tired from their ordeal. "What do you guys think?"

"I say leave no stone unturned," her dad said determinedly.

Andrea had just opened her mouth to answer when she saw a blonde teenager with a sign under her arm step out to cross the road behind them.

That girl looks like Bethany, she thought to herself. Then the girl turned to make sure the coast was clear, and Andrea saw that she had only one arm.

It *was* Bethany!

"That's her! That's her!" she said excitedly. "That's Bethany!"

Just as the driver turned the limo around, Andrea saw Bethany hand the sign off to a woman and hop into a waiting car that drove off.

"Oh, no!" Andrea and her mom said at the same time.

"Maybe that woman can tell us where to find her," Andrea's dad suggested, sounding as disappointed as Andrea felt.

They hurried across the parking lot towards the young blonde woman who was now rolling up signs and putting them in the back of her SUV. Other than her, there was no one else around.

"Excuse me," Andrea said, trying to remain calm.

"Yes?" the woman straightened up, shielding her eyes from the sun as she took in the family, as well as the limo. "Can I help you?"

"I was looking for a girl named Bethany ... and her friend Holly. At least I think that's her name."

"You mean Bethany Hamilton and Holly Silva?"

"I ... I mean we ... we don't know their last names ... but how many could there be?"

The woman smiled at Andrea. "Holly is dark haired and about so high." She raised her hand to approximately Andrea's height. "And Bethany is tall and blonde with only one arm?"

Andrea looked back at her mom and grinned. "That's them!"

"I'm sorry, we should introduce ourselves and explain why we are looking for them," Andrea's mom interjected. Then she rushed on to tell the woman their story; how they had gotten into trouble on the Hanakapiai Trail, and how the girls had come to their aid.

"We wanted to meet with them before we left," Andrea's dad added. "And I really wanted to give them some sort of reward ... to show my gratitude."

"You know, I am sure that they would be happy to meet you, but they won't take a reward. I know those girls well." The woman smiled prettily. "They would say that they were just doing what God would have wanted them to do."

Andrea and her mom smiled at each other.

"Well, there must be something we could do for them!" Andrea's dad persisted. "I realize that you don't know me, but I'm telling you that I feel very strongly that I want to do something for these girls!"

The young woman looked at Andrea's dad for a long moment and then nodded to herself—as if some sort of decision had been made.

"Well, there just might be something you could help them with after all."

seven

Bethany stood at the edge of the beach and gazed happily at the crowd that was quickly forming for the surf-a-thon fundraiser with inflatables.

She couldn't have asked for a nicer day. A few traces of puffy white clouds were pushed along by gentle trade winds as the sun glinted off the waves that were rolling in, promising a fun, easy surf.

A short distance away, her youth group stood in clusters around a huge array of silly inflatable pool toys: whales, turtles, sharks, and dolphins. There was also a queen-sized air mattress, old black inner tubes, small boats, and even an inflatable kiddie-sized swimming pool.

Bethany smiled as she listened to her friends in the youth group laughing as they each picked their "ride." Most of the boys lunged for the sharks or whales. *Big surprise*, Bethany thought, shaking her head. Monica took the air mattress, while Holly and Malia opted for the inner tubes. Jenna grabbed up a boat and then turned and waved at Bethany. Even from where she stood, she could see the excitement in their faces.

It was so crazy, it just might work!

Bethany stacked the sponsor forms in a neat pile and glanced towards the parking lot. She could see Sarah being approached by some more people. She said a quick prayer that God would bless their day and that somehow, someway, they would meet their goal.

You never know how God is going to work it all out, Sarah's voice whispered through her memory. Bethany smiled to herself. If she had learned anything over the past couple of days, it was that. While she didn't know *how* God would work it out, she knew he would ... in his own way.

Bethany caught sight of her brothers on the beach. They were both busy setting up cameras like they did with her regular surf contests. Noah took his spot on the beach while Tim was preparing to shoot water shots with an underwater housing. Bethany picked up the little kiddie pool she'd be riding and headed in their direction.

"What's with all of the cameras *today?*" Bethany asked.

"This is hilarious," Noah answered with a grin. "And I think some of the sponsors who can't be here would definitely like a copy of what happens today. I know I do."

Bethany grinned back. "So, you like the idea of me looking like a nut ball, riding the waves in this kiddie pool?"

"Well ... when you put it like that ... yeah!"

"Best idea I've heard in a long time," Tim added, and Bethany laughed.

Sarah suddenly appeared on the beach with sunglasses, a huge straw hat, and a stack of forms on her clipboard. She called everyone together.

"Okay you guys! Here is the objective—should you choose to take it—ride as many waves as you can in an hour's time. You will have to count the waves yourselves, so be honest. When you are done, report the number to me. I will fill out your sponsor sheets, and you can collect your money. I know that some of you were given pledges already, and we have all that tracked. So go on out and have a great time!"

With that, she blew a whistle, and Bethany, the Hanalei girls, and the rest of their youth group grabbed up their inflatables and ran into the surf.

It was a sight to see. And that's putting it mildly.

Visitors and locals alike cracked up over the comic menagerie of inflatable animals hurtling down the face of the waves, and in some cases they were so out of control that they mowed down anyone in their path.

Air mattresses—not meant for dropping down the face of a wave—pitched many of their laughing riders off into the cushion of white water.

Wave after wave, the white water washed in a bizarre array of floating pool toys with teenagers barely hanging on. At the shore, the riders picked up their beasts and ran back for another round.

At the end of the hour Sarah blew her whistle, and the crowd came in laughing and telling stories of wipeouts, crashes, and mow downs.

After the students reported to Sarah the number of waves caught, they attacked their ice chests and waited for the results.

A few minutes later, Sarah gathered the group around her. "Okay, great job, guys! We had people sponsor rides for a quarter a ride up to five bucks a ride. But we had one sponsor in particular"—and here she glanced over at Bethany and Holly—"who has made it possible for us to go on our trip without any more fundraisers."

Bethany and Holly high-fived each other as the youth group hooted and cheered around them.

"It's like a miracle," Monica said to no one in particular.

"These folks sponsored Bethany and Holly for one ride only," Sarah went on with a big smile. The noise died down as everyone, especially Bethany and Holly, suddenly looked at Sarah in confusion.

"They put down $2,500 for each girl's first wave! We made it gang! We're going to Mexico!"

Cheers broke out again, and kids slapped each other on the back—all except for Bethany and Holly, who were looking at each other dumbfounded.

"You know something I don't know?" Bethany asked, and Holly shook her head.

"I know I didn't have sponsorship like *that*!"

"Me either. Something's gotta be wrong," Bethany said. And they both turned to see Sarah's beaming face.

"You two were sponsored by someone who feels like they owe you a lot more than that for what you did for them."

The girls looked at each other, still puzzled.

"Forgotten your little Hanakapiai adventure so soon?" Sarah prodded.

"I don't get it," Bethany said. Holly's look mirrored hers.

"The folks you helped off the mountain wanted to say thank you," Sarah explained finally. "They had to go home already, but they left a couple letters for you."

With that, Sarah handed the girls two thank-you notes from Andrea and Susan.

"No way!" Bethany said, looking down at the thick envelope in her hand. She thought of the winding trail that had led her to this moment. She was overwhelmed; no way could she have mapped out something like this. She glanced up at Holly, tears in her eyes.

"You never know how God is going to work it all out," Bethany said softly, almost to herself, and then shook her head in wonder.

"And sometimes you don't see the clues he left until the end of the mystery," Holly said with a smile. "We sure didn't see this coming!"

"But you were both faithful and listened to him lead you," Sarah added.

"It makes me wonder where he is going to lead us next!" Bethany exclaimed. "I have a feeling our 'mystery' isn't over yet!"

eight

Bethany dug her toes into the sand as she and Holly watched the small waves roll onto the beach. The forecasted swell hadn't materialized to nearly the size that was promised, but it had been a fun day of surfing anyway, and neither of them felt like packing it in just yet. At least Bethany didn't. She took in a deep breath, smelling sun and salt.

There was something about the ocean, the sound of the crashing waves, the breeze—no matter where she was, it always drew her back. Kind of like a favorite song she never got tired of hearing.

Bethany smiled.

Like that Switchfoot song she and Holly sang at the top of their lungs along Hanakapiai Trail. They had totally wrecked the song, but at least it had caught Andrea's attention. She shook her head at the memory, and then an idea suddenly hit her.

"Wanna try something new?" she asked out of the blue, and then grinned as Holly narrowed her green eyes at her, already suspicious.

"Like what? You've almost killed me twice now with those new ideas of yours."

Bethany laughed.

"All right, so what's your idea of fun today?" Holly asked in spite of herself.

"Switch foot," Bethany said as she grabbed up her board and headed for the water.

"The band?" Holly asked, grabbing her own board as she hurried to catch up.

"No, silly! Doing what the band is named for; switching feet. We'll surf the opposite of our normal way." As if to make her point, she quickly bent over and strapped her leash onto her right ankle.

"I'm probably going to regret this," Holly said, strapping her leash onto her left ankle.

"Maybe, but no switching back," Bethany grinned. "Deal?"

"Deal!"

The girls plunged into the warm water and paddled through the foam, past the impact zone, to the deep, clear water.

"Seems like a long wait between set waves," Bethany said as they bobbed on their surfboards, looking for a discolored line in the horizon.

"There it is!" Holly said, gearing up for the approaching wave.

Digging in with her powerful right arm, Bethany was first out, easily catching the small wave. Then she found herself wobbling a little as she got to her feet and tried to plant her right foot over the tail of the surfboard. The micro-second delay in timing caused her to flounder behind a cascade of white water, and the section of the wave she would have normally conquered broke in front of her.

Bethany laughed and kicked her board away as she tossed herself backwards into the white water.

Holly caught the next wave and immediately fumbled at the takeoff point as she tried to get her footing. The nose of the board dug under the water and flipped her headfirst off the board. Bethany could hear Holly laughing as she paddled towards her at the lineup.

"I couldn't even make the section!" Bethany grinned as she swiped her hair out of her eyes.

"I pearled up to my neck and went over the falls!" Holly laughed breathlessly. "It's a good thing we're leaving for Mexico soon, so I can hide out there with my wounded ego."

"Oh, there's not gonna be any hiding—we have houses to build!" Bethany wagged her finger at Holly and then paddled back out to catch another wave.

Wave after wave, the pair struggled to master surfing with a switch-foot stance. They took more than their fair share of drubbings in the white water, but by the end of the session, both Bethany and Holly had become fairly good at charging waves wrong foot forward. And both stuck to their agreement not to change back—even though they drooled over some beautiful little tubes that popped up while they practiced their new stance.

"One more and we've gotta go!" Bethany called out finally. "Tim will be here soon, and you know how he loves to wait!"

Both girls quickly grabbed the first small waves that came along and rode them all the way to the beach.

"Whose crazy idea was that?" Bethany laughed breathlessly.

"Actually, it was kind of fun after a while," Holly admitted. "But the first few waves were *brutal!*"

"I wouldn't have suggested it if the waves were good," Bethany said.

"I wouldn't have agreed if the waves were good!" Holly countered, and they both laughed.

Bethany let the cool water wash away the salt from her hair as she stood under the outdoor shower at the beach park and listened to Holly slaughter another favorite song of theirs in the stall next to her.

No way am I joining in on that, she thought with a grin. *My luck, Tim would show up and have a tape recorder on him.*

The singing suddenly stopped, and she heard Holly turn the water off in her stall.

"Bethany?"

"Um, yeah?"

"I was just thinking. Surfing switch foot ... is that how you felt right after the shark attack? Like your body was used to one way and then had to learn another entirely different way?"

Bethany glanced at the wall between them, caught off guard by Holly's question. "You know, I never really thought about it like that, but yeah, that is kind of how I felt."

They both dressed quickly and met each other outside. Holly smiled shyly at Bethany. "Sorry for being nosy, but I was just wondering if you ever felt that way now?"

"You're not nosy, you're Holly!" Bethany joked, trying to make light of the question, and—if she was going to be honest—kind of avoiding the answer. Truth was, Holly had asked something that had been in the back of her mind a lot lately.

God guiding her and giving her strength like he did on Hanakapiai Trail had made her feel a lot better about things. God seemed to give her what she needed when she needed it. But there were times when something would come up to painfully remind her that she had lost her arm ... and she would wonder again why it had to happen.

Bethany raised her eyes to meet Holly's. "Yeah, I guess there are times when I still feel that way," she admitted a little reluctantly. The understanding and friendship she saw in Holly's eyes helped her to go on. "I guess I've thought about it even more since we found out we're going to Mexico soon."

"But I thought you couldn't wait to go!"

"I started thinking about how cool it would be to go on a mission trip with Sarah and the youth group way before I lost my arm," Bethany said as they walked over to a park bench and sat down.

Holly looked at her, confused.

Bethany managed a small smile. "So, it hits me right after the surf-a-thon that we're really going to Mexico … and I start thinking of how much more I could do down there if I hadn't lost my arm."

Holly nodded and then frowned. "It's kind of weird that you would be thinking this stuff right after all the cool stuff God did through you on Hanaka-piai Trail, isn't it?"

"Yeah, I thought about that too."

"I know it's got to be hard," Holly said. "I mean, I don't get why it happened to you. I see lots of people that are real jerks and they get good jobs, lots of money, handsome boyfriends—all that stuff. Then I think about you, and I wonder why."

"Are you saying I'm not a jerk?" Bethany laughed and then sobered a little. "I wondered why too. But my dad helped me with that."

"What did he say?"

"He said I might not understand the answer even if God gave it to me."

"I don't get it."

"He said it's kind of like when parents take their baby to the doctor to get a shot. The baby is totally freaked out and doesn't understand why her mom or dad is holding her down for the scary doctor to put a sharp needle in her leg or arm. Because the baby is too little to understand, she can't see the love in her parents' actions. She wonders why they are putting her through it. And even if they told her about viruses, bacteria, and all that, she still wouldn't understand."

"That makes sense," Holly nodded. "I guess you just gotta have faith and trust God. Kind of like what you did on the trail; letting him be strong when you felt weak."

"Exactly."

"But that doesn't mean it's easy."

"You got it."

"Do you think life is always going to be this hard?" Holly said dramatically.

"Probably," Bethany said.

Sleep didn't come for awhile that night as Bethany lay in her bed thinking about her conversation with Holly—thinking about *all* that had happened in such a short period of time.

In spite of all her worries and insecurities, her stubbornness at times, and even her doubts, God had still spoken to her—used her to touch another life—and that amazed her more than anything she had ever known or seen. She glanced over at Andrea's letter lying open next to her and smiled at the words that stood out like a beacon from the page:

> *There aren't many people who can say they witnessed a miracle, so it's*

probably going to take some getting used to—especially for me who had never even prayed before that day. It's kind of like joining a club that you just learned about and being made president all in one day. But I guess you know all of this already. The fact that you lived through that shark attack must have been one of those major, run-around-the-ballpark-and-make-a-homerun kind of miracles that had people in heaven jumping to their feet and cheering. God knew you had a dream.

So do I. You probably won't guess it, so I'll just tell you: I want to be a writer. So, thank you, Bethany, for being the answer to my prayer. Because you were brave enough to trust God, I have a chance at that dream of mine.

I'm still learning the ropes on this praying stuff, but I want you to know I'm going to be praying for you— praying that God will continue to help you reach out to others. From what I hear, it sounds like Mexico will be your next journey!

Andrea

Bethany curled her toes under Ginger's warm body snuggled at the foot of the bed and looked around her room. Funny how after the dust had settled from the Hanakapiai Trail rescue and the surf-a-thon, she felt God was still talking to her through Sarah, Holly, and now this letter from Andrea ...

The door of her bedroom suddenly opened, and Bethany sat up to see her mom and dad peeking in. Not their usual deal, but *okay* ...

"We just thought we'd check in on you before we go to bed," her dad said. "Everything okay?"

"Better than okay," Bethany answered and then yawned, suddenly feeling tired.

"We love you, honey," Bethany's mom added. "Everything's been so rushed around here lately that we haven't even had the chance to tell you how happy we are for you about the mission trip."

"Thank you," she said sleepily as they shut her door. She flopped back against her pillows and sighed. Then something suddenly occurred to her about her parent's little visit. God was speaking to her through her parents. She smiled.

"I love you too, God."

Dear Bethany,

You might be shocked when I say your letter about God leading you to that girl trapped on the cliff didn't surprise me—but it didn't. It wasn't that long ago that you and Malia met someone else that needed rescuing ... on a little island called Samoa. Remember?

I wasn't hanging off a cliff, but I felt like I was ready to go over the ledge—if you know what I mean.

But I think that's what God does for all of us. He meets us on whatever kind of ledge we're on. The good news is he doesn't leave us there.

The bad news (if you want to look at it as bad) is that he does sometimes call us to face or do some things that we wouldn't normally do.

If I could give you one thing to take on your mission trip, it would be these words to think on: "The heart of a man plans his way, but the Lord establishes his steps."—Proverbs 16:9

Your friend,

Liam

P.S. Write me and let me know when you're coming home. You never know,

I might just show up sometime and challenge you to another surfing contest!

one

Bethany felt a jolt of nervous excitement as the airplane's tires hit the runway in Los Angeles. Then she glanced at the bundle of nerves sitting in the seat next to her and grinned. If there was *anyone* who understood how she was feeling at that moment, it was Holly Silva. They not only surfed together and trained together, they also survived cliff-hanging rescues together. And *that* was a bonding moment if there ever was one.

"So, what do you think?"

Holly gave her a shaky grin. "Guess I was having a hard time believing this was for real, until now."

"Yeah ... I still can't believe we're finally on our first mission trip," Bethany said, filled with awe as she scanned the other excited faces on the plane. The usual suspects were there: Malia, Jenna, and Monica were craning their necks to catch a glimpse of Bethany and Holly who sat a couple of rows behind. They spotted them and waved wildly, causing them to laugh.

"All of us in Mexico. This is going to be crazy!" Bethany shook her head.

"Good crazy, right?" Holly asked tentatively, and they both laughed again as Bethany continued to look around.

Black spiky hair gave Kai's location away as he gabbed with his buddies, including Dano, a large teenager with cool tribal tattoos. *A giant heart to match too,* Bethany thought, remembering how hard he had worked on the fund-raisers.

Kai said something that brought a roar of laughter from the guys, and Bethany couldn't help smiling to herself. *Not exactly your typical church youth group*, she thought. But then, that was kind of the cool thing about their group.

None of them were exactly typical.

Oh, there were some like her who came from strong Christian families, but the majority of teens peering out the windows of the 747 at the orange lights flickering from the "City of Angels" were from homes where the name of Christ was more likely used in a curse than in praise.

But that didn't seem to stop them from reaching out to God—something she could totally identify with.

Kai and Dano had been drawn to their group by the wild and crazy game night Sarah and her staff had put together, but they stayed because somewhere along the way they found out Jesus was for real.

Bethany smiled to herself, remembering how blown away they all were the day their miracle financial gift appeared, allowing them to go on this mission trip.

After countless car washes and even after her crazy idea of a surf-a-thon with inflatable toys, they were still such a long way off from what they needed that a lot of them wondered if the mission trip was really going to happen. And then God showed up in his perfect time to make it possible.

No one had any doubts after that happened that God was behind them on the trip—or that he was paving the way for something good to happen.

The Fasten Seat Belt signs turned off overhead, and she and Holly, along with everyone else on the plane, scrambled for their carry-on bags.

"Okay, everyone, stick together and meet us at the gate!" Sarah, their youth director, called out before she followed her assistants, Mike and Gabe, off the plane.

"I wonder what it's going to be like," Holly said as the group fanned out along the boarding tunnel. Bethany glanced over at her. Short, trendy hair, just a touch of lipstick (a recent victory in her makeup battle with her mom)—Holly looked cute and sure of herself, but Bethany knew Holly was just as nervous as she was ... if not more.

"Guess we'll find out soon enough," Bethany smiled, trying to sound more confident than she felt.

"Ghettos aren't pretty, that's for sure," Jenna said.

"I hear some of the stuff we're going to do is pretty harsh," Malia said as she slung a backpack over her shoulder.

"Great!" Monica said, giving her new manicure a worried look.

"Well, *I'm* game," Bethany announced.

"When *aren't you* game?" Kai teased, looking over his shoulder as they entered the terminal. "Car washes, surf-a-thons ..." He glanced over at Dano and winked. "No telling what she'll come up with for us to do in Mexico."

"Be afraid," Holly said with a mischievous grin.

"*Very* afraid," Bethany added, and they all laughed.

Thirty minutes later, they were piling into the three vans idling by the curb in the early-morning light. Sarah, Mike, and Gabe were in the drivers' seats.

In spite of the all-night flight, Bethany found her mind racing, wondering about the week to come. Unlike her friends, whose heads were already bobbing back to sleep as soon as the vans hit the interstate, she had slept through most of the flight. She was used to traveling at odd hours for surf competitions.

She turned and squinted out the window at the California scenery flashing by. She thought about Sarah's description of some of the work they would be doing in the ghettos that lined the deep hills and gullies around Tijuana: building small houses, bathing children from areas without running water, playing with orphans, and handing out food and clothes.

More scenery flashed by as Bethany stared out the window and thought about Jesus' words: "When you help them, you help me." She thought how cool it was that Jesus wanted the world to know how much he loved people who were, for the most part, forgotten or ignored.

She knew God had given her a heart that wanted to reach out to people. She just hoped she measured up now that she was in the position to help.

Bethany suddenly sat up straight as the Pacific Ocean came into view. "That's Trestles!" she said excitedly, elbowing Holly. "They're holding the nationals there this week."

"Wha—?" Holly mumbled groggily.

Kai cracked an eye open and asked, "So, why aren't you there? Or is that a sore subject?"

"Not *too* sore," Bethany admitted with an unconvincing grin.

"All things work together for good, right?" Malia said with a sleepy, but warm smile. Bethany glanced over at her, remembering their surf trip in Samoa.

"Yeah ... if I had qualified, I wouldn't be on this trip."

"Could've saved us a lot of work," Kai said, grinning at Dano. But Dano was still sleeping soundly.

Soon the others fell back to sleep, and Bethany continued to watch the California coastline as the vans continued south toward San Diego and the Mexican border.

By the time they reached the United States-Mexico border, most of the kids were awake. The border crossing went pretty smoothly, but the sudden change at the border from the US side to the hardscrabble town pressed up against the edge of a large steel fence shocked many of the kids into silence.

It seems like we've stepped into another world, Bethany thought. With no trees and with cement everywhere, it looked so barren. But almost immediately they entered the busy city traffic of Tijuana.

"Whoa! This is *nuts!*" Sarah said about the crazy traffic. Cars zoomed around her on both sides, while she tried to keep up with Mike and Gabe in the vans ahead. She glanced in the rearview mirror with an exasperated sigh.

"Hey, Sarah, maybe you should let me take over from here," Kai suggested.

"Or me," Dano piped up. "I know all about nuts."

"Uh-huh," Sarah smiled, trying to keep her eyes on the road.

"Yeah, they're real experts," Bethany added, trying to keep a straight face as they bantered back and forth.

They flashed past dozens of tiny eateries and stands that sold anything you could imagine, from fresh spices to wild-looking guitars to jewelry, clothes, and beautiful pottery. People were everywhere. Color was everywhere. Bethany spotted an enormous fruit market and felt her mouth water.

"If we get the chance, I'm so there," Bethany said.

"Look at those cool skirts!" Holly said.

"Where?" Monica asked, practically trying to crawl over Malia and Jenna for a peek. The girls groaned in unison and then laughed.

"Monica, you're too much," Jenna chuckled.

"What? So I like clothes. What girl doesn't?"

"This isn't exactly going to be fashion week in New York," Bethany teased as the vans turned down an old dusty road, slowing to a stop in front of a slightly crumbling but tidy-looking two-story building.

"Not exactly Kansas either, Dorothy," Kai said under his breath as they all took in the iron bars on every window. A wild-looking dog peered at them from the side of the dusty, dinged up SUV parked next to the building.

"Wow," Bethany said, feeling her nervousness return as she looked at the poverty around them. She felt her spirits rise again at the sight of a friendly looking couple exiting the house to greet them.

"Okay, gang, let's go meet our hosts," Sarah said with a smile as she pulled her keys from the ignition.

"Come on, Toto," Bethany called over her shoulder to Kai as she, Holly, and the other girls scrambled for the door. Dano's laughter followed them out of the van.

Eddie and Maggie Passmore were about as nice as you could get, Bethany thought as Maggie pulled away from hugging her and Eddie grabbed her hand in a warm, energetic handshake. She'd been the last in line for the welcome, but they didn't seem to have lost their enthusiasm.

"So, are you ready for the tour?" Eddie asked with a broad smile.

"Oh, she's ready," Kai said dryly as Eddie led them into a large room filled with a mismatch of used sofas and chairs parked on a worn but clean carpet.

"Our strategy room," Eddie provided. "It's not exactly the Hilton, but it works."

"What made you pick Mexico?" Bethany asked as he led them out of the main room to the lower part of the dorm that held the office and a kitchen large enough for visiting groups to prepare meals.

"I first visited here when I was a teenager," he replied, glancing around at the group. "Probably about Kai and Dano's age—you two are about sixteen, right?" The boys nodded. "It really got in my blood. I mean, no matter where I went after that, through college to being a youth pastor ... I just couldn't get these people out of my mind. The next time I visited with Maggie, God opened the doors for us in such a big way that there was no doubt *where* he wanted us." Eddie smiled and shook his head, giving Maggie a look that said it still amazed him.

"Let's show them where they'll be sleeping," Maggie said with a smile of her own as she led the tired but curious group upstairs.

The upper part of the dorm was divided into two large sleeping areas; one for guys and one for girls, with shower facilities for both. Duffel bags began to drop around them like flies as Bethany and the girls rushed to claim the bunks they wanted. They laughed, hearing the commotion from the boys' side. They could hear Mike say, "Come on, guys, age has priority!"

"How much you want to bet Dano gets whatever bunk he wants?" Bethany grinned.

"If I was as big as a giant, I know I'd get the bunk I wanted," Holly said as she flopped onto her bed. "I feel like I could sleep forever."

"Me too," Malia yawned.

"Not me," Monica said. "This neighborhood makes me nervous."

"Getting your nails done makes you nervous," Jenna said, and Monica threw a pillow at her.

"Well, there's no way I can sleep yet. I'm going to see if I can find Sarah," Bethany said, rising from her bunk.

"Don't volunteer me for anything crazy until you, like, *ask* me first," Holly called after her as she headed for the door.

"That goes double for the rest of us," Malia said, getting nods of agreement from Jenna and Monica.

"Are you talking to me?" Bethany said as she blinked innocently and then hurried to shut the door behind her before anyone could respond.

Chuckling to herself, she jogged down the stairs, turned the corner, and almost ran right into Eddie as he rounded the corner from the opposite direction. They both laughed.

"Almost a head-on collision," Eddie said, grinning.

"Oh man, you aren't kidding!" She glanced behind Eddie. "I was looking for Sarah. Have you seen her?"

Eddie nodded. "As a matter of fact, Maggie took her on a tour of the neighborhood."

"I was going to ask her if we could go running tomorrow morning."

"You mean your whole group?"

"Well, probably just us girls," Bethany said, then chewed on her lip thoughtfully. "Or at the very least, me and Holly." She grinned inwardly. *Sorry, Holly!*

"You're a surfer, right?"

"Yeah," Bethany nodded shyly. "I kind of like to keep up on my training." She left out the part about running helping her nerves over the mission trip.

"Nothing wrong with that," Eddie said amiably. "I used to run myself—though it's been a while." He patted his stomach, and Bethany smiled.

"Tell you what: it's not that great of a neighborhood for you girls to go running in alone. But if you really want to go, I'll come around 6:30 a.m. and run with you."

"Really? You don't mind?"

"Maggie will thank you; she's been after me to get back into running. I'm still carrying around all the stuff I ate at Christmastime."

"Okay then, it's a deal," Bethany said happily. "I'll set the alarm on my watch."

"Don't forget the time change. And I'll bring the stick."

"A stick? What for?"

"Ah, if you're going to go for a jog around here, carrying a stick with you is a good idea."

"For muggers?" Bethany asked worriedly. Holly might forgive her for an early morning run, but not for a mugger.

"Yeah ... the *four-legged* kind," Eddie laughed. "The stray dogs around here can sometimes get a little too close for comfort."

Bethany nodded casually, but her mind raced. *What have I got us into now, Holly?* she thought with a twinge of doubt—not just about the run—but the whole trip. Then she remembered her dad's words just before she got on the plane: "Just trust in God and let him lead you, Bethany. He's the best father any of us could ever imagine having."

"Papa!"

Eduardo shot up from the pallet he had been sleeping on and looked around. It was dark, but he knew if he reached out his arm he could touch the cot his mother and sister slept on, knew that the other two cots his four brothers shared would be just beyond that. He put his hand to his chest, feeling his heart still racing from the dream. And what a good dream it was!

He had been running down a beautiful soccer field. So much green! He had never seen that much green in one place. He grinned to himself, remembering how he scored a goal for his team and how good it felt when his teammates thumped his back with congratulations. His smile faded as he recalled searching for his father's face in the stand filled with people.

For just a moment, he thought he'd spotted him when he saw a man stand up and begin to walk toward him through the crowd. But people kept getting in his way, and no matter how hard

Eduardo squinted, he couldn't make out the man's face.

Eduardo shivered but resisted the urge to crawl onto his mother's cot. If his brothers woke up and saw him there, he would never hear the end of it. They would say he was *loco* to dream that he would do anything other than rummage through other people's garbage. They would also say that he was a baby to call out to a father he had never had.

Eduardo grimaced and curled up on his pallet again. He wasn't a baby. He was five years old—old enough to know better than to wake his mother, and old enough to know he needed some sleep before he had to get up and go to work again.

Still, he thought as his eyes began to grow heavy with sleep, it would have been nice if he could have seen that man's face. It would be nice to at least *pretend* he had a father.

Soul Surfer series
Rise Above
A 90-Day Devotional
CHECK OUT
this excerpt from
another book in the
Soul Surfer Series.
Bethany Hamilton
with Doris Rikkers
zonderkidz

Devotion 1
Big Plans Ahead

On that October morning of the shark attack, everyone around me (including me!) feared that my plans for being a professional surfer were over. Who had ever heard of a surfer with one arm? How would I paddle out? How would I get up on the board? How would I balance? All the hopes and dreams about surfing that I'd had since I was little seemed to be gone.

But you know what? God had plans for me. He had bigger plans than I could have ever imagined. Before the attack, I might have become a surfer and been well-known in the surfing crowd. I might have had my picture on several surfing magazines. But now God is able to use me in a different way, above and beyond all that I could ever ask or think. He's doing things in my life that I could never have dreamed of before the attack. He's helping me to rise above it all.

God has big plans for your life too. The purpose he has for your life is different than the one he has for mine. But he's got plans. Big plans. You need to be willing to be used by him. Trust him. Follow him. Ask him to start preparing your heart for his purpose.

God's Words Inspire

"For I know the plans I have for you," declares the LORD, *"plans to prosper you and not to harm you, plans to give you hope and a future."*

—Jeremiah 29:11

Chatting with God

Dear God, thank you for having a plan for me. Help me to trust that your plan for my future is the best for me. Give me patience and help me to prepare for what you have in store for me. In Jesus' name, amen.

Did You Know?

Jeremiah 29:11 is one of my favorite Bible verses. My youth counselor, Sarah, was inspired by God to think of it the morning she heard about the attack. It's been a great support for me, my family, and my friends ever since.

Devotion 2
Rock Solid Foundation

I've spent my whole life enjoying the ocean, the surf, and the sand on the beach. I know all about sand castles and the surf. I've seen how one wave can just wipe out a sand castle in a second. Houses, castles, dreams, or plans only last if they are built on a solid foundation. God is the rock in my life—my foundation. I keep my relationship with him strong.

It's good to have dreams. I hope you have lots of dreams to do spectacular things. But you have to put your hope and faith into something that can't suddenly disappear. You need a strong foundation, a hard rock platform to build your dreams and future plans upon. Anything less than that will be a total wipeout.

Popularity can be lost with one round of gossip. Money can be easily taken away or lost. Clothes go out of style. Nothing really lasts except God's love. If you build your hopes and dreams and your life on him, you'll always be on solid ground and able to survive life's challenges.

God's Words Inspire

Therefore everyone who hears these words of mine and puts them into practice is like a wise man who built his house on the rock. The rain came down, the streams rose, and the winds blew and beat against that house; yet it did not fall, because it had its foundation on the rock.

—Matthew 7:24–5

Chatting with God

Jesus, help me to put my faith in you. Help me build my life upon you, my Rock, so I will be strong and secure in you. In Jesus' name, amen.

Did You Know?

Have you ever picked up a handful of sand and tried to count the grains? Have you noticed all the different color variations and seen how it sparkles when the sun shines on it? It's made from the earth's elements of the area it's in: coral, shells, rock, sandstone, quartz, etc. There are even beaches with all black sand from volcanic rock. How precious are God's thoughts toward us that they are more in number than the grains of sand on the beach (Psalm 139:17–18).

Devotion 3
Faithful Friends

One of the greatest gifts God has given me is my friends. One of my dearest friends is Alana, my surfing buddy. Alana was surfing with me when I got attacked by the shark. She stayed with me through the whole thing. She's awesome!

I have a big *ohana* of friends too: friends from my church, friends from the community, and friends from the surfing world. Then there's my tight group of personal friends. These are the friends who will love me no matter what. They loved me with two arms, and they love me now with one arm. My friends have been the greatest to help me through the tough times. They've made me laugh and feel normal again.

God wants us to be Christlike in our relationships with our friends. He wants us to be a friend others can trust and receive encouragement from—not condemnation or criticism. Jesus is the best friend you could ever have. He wants only what is best for us. He gives us guidance in his Word for our safety and protection. He

promises to never leave us or forsake us. Real friends
are like Jesus. They shine with Jesus' love. I hope you
will be a friend like that.

God's Words Inspire

A friend loves at all times.
        —Proverbs 17:17

Chatting with God

Dear Jesus, thank you for being my very best
friend. Thank you for the friends I have in my life
right now. Help me to be a faithful friend whom
others can trust. Help me to be a friend who
forgives, encourages, loves, and laughs with
others. In Jesus' name, amen.

Did You Know?

Ohana is a Hawaiian word that means
"family unit or close group."

Soul Surfer series
Ask Bethany
FAQ's: Surfing, Faith & Friends
CHECK OUT this excerpt from Bethany Hamilton's FAQ book, Ask Bethany
Bethany Hamilton
with Doris Rikkers
zonderkidz

Bethany Basics

Q. It has been a long time since I have seen your picture. What do you look like now?

Q. How tall are you?

A. I'm taller now than I was when I was attacked by the shark. I was 5'7" when I was 13, but now I'm 5' 10". I have blond hair and hazel eyes and an Irish–Norwegian heritage.

Q. How old are you?

A. I'm 16 years old now while I'm writing this.

Q. When is your birthday?

A. I was born February 8, 1990.

Q. Where do you live?

A. I live in the town of Princeville, on the north shore of the island of Kauai, in the state of Hawaii, in the middle of the Pacific Ocean.

Q. Were you born in Hawaii or someplace else?

A. I was born in Hawaii, on the island of Kauai, in the emergency room at Wilcox Memorial Hospital.

Q. Where do you go to school?

A. I now stay home to go to school—
that sounds funny, doesn't it?
Anyway, I went to Hanalei Elementary
School in the town of Hanalei, on
Kauai. I started homeschooling after
sixth grade so I'd have more time to
surf. I do my studies through American
School. They have students all over the
world! I pretty much *have* to homeschool
these days because I travel so much.

Q. Are you a Christian?

A. Yes, I am. I believe in Jesus Christ as my
Lord and Savior and my God. I have a
personal relationship with God through
Jesus Christ. For more about my faith see
the chapter "About Faith."

Q. When did you become a Christian?

A. I've been a Christian for as long as I
can remember. I was about five when
I recognized Jesus as my Savior and
committed to follow him, love him, and live
my life for him!

Q. Where do you go to church?

A. I go to the North Shore Community
Church near my home.

Q. What color is your hair?

A. I have medium length, straight blonde hair. It looks just like my mom's hair did when she was my age.

Q. I heard you have blonde hair. Is that your natural color? Do you use peroxide or anything on it?

A. My hair is thin, so it naturally bleaches out from the sun even more than most people's hair. I like everything real and natural, so I don't use artificial products and I try to avoid chemicals as much as possible.

Q. I heard you're really cute, so I checked out some of the pics on the Web. Sure enough, you are. Life's not fair. How come you're cute and popular, and I'm not?

A. God makes us the way we are for a reason and he never makes a mistake. You were designed with his perfect love! We just have to make the best of what we've got. And besides, it's what's inside us that really counts. Kindness and love are more important than looks. My mom has me look up words in the Strong's Concordance to find their deeper meaning. I found out that real beauty is more valuable if it's inside our hearts. *Grace*, *pleasant*, *agreeable*, *precious*, *delight*, *honor*, and *godly* were a few of the words that were a part of being beautiful. Sin is what really makes a person look ugly, so be beautiful with a clean heart!

On the Same Wave

Here's what the Bible tells us about outward appearance:

The LORD said to Samuel, "Do not consider his appearance or his height… The LORD does not look at the things man looks at. Man looks at the outward appearance, but the LORD looks at the heart."

—1 Samuel 16:7

Beauty is more about what's on the inside than what's on the outside.

Your beauty should not come from outward adornment… Instead, it should be that of your inner self, the unfading beauty of a gentle and quiet spirit, which is of great worth in God's sight."

—1 Peter 3:3–4

Q. What's your middle name?

A. Meilani, which means "heavenly flower."

Q. Do you have a nickname, or does everybody call you Bethany?

A. Bebo, B-ham, or Bethy.

Q. What's your favorite holiday?

A. Valentine's Day

Q. Who's your favorite movie star?

A. I don't really have one, but I like to laugh, so I'd say either John Heder, who plays Napoleon Dynamite, or the actor who plays Dewey in *Malcolm in the Middle*.

Q. Do you have any pets? If yes, what are their names?

Q. What kind of pets do you have?

A. I have a dog, a shar-pei named Ginger. She's the most adorable little dog you'll ever see! She's been in our family for years. I used to have a horse named Koko. My mom sold her because she took too much time away from surfing, and she bucked too much.

Q. Do you take your pets with you when you travel?

A. No. Ginger hates water, so she doesn't like to go to the beach. We even had to get her a raincoat so we could walk her. (It rains a lot here.)

Q. Who takes care of your dog when you're gone?

A. There's usually somebody in my family still back at home—my dad or one of my brothers. My entire family doesn't come along when I travel. So someone is home to take care of things, including my dog.

Q. Do you drive yet?

Q. Do you have your driver's license?

A. Yes, I just got my driver's license! In the summer of 2006 I finally passed the test, and now I can drive myself to the beach and Bible study!!!

Q. What grade are you in?

A. I'm in my junior year of high school. That would be the eleventh grade. For more about school, see the chapter "School and Other Stuff".

Q. What will you do after high school?

A. I'm not sure yet. I have so many things that I'd like to do, but my first priority will be pro surfing. I'd like to travel to contests all over the world. Also, at the same time I can study the Bible on my travels and get an online degree or something. I love photography, so I'll try to learn about that too! For more on the future, see the chapter "What's Happening Next."

Crunch

Written by Rick Bundschuh,
Inspired by Bethany Hamilton

Fiction • Softcover • ISBN 0-310-71225-4

On a trip to Mexico Bethany
meets a soccer-loving little
boy who captures her heart in
an unexpected way. Because
of a promise she makes him,
Bethany's competition in a
prestigious surf contest is
threatened.

Soul Surfer series

Available now at your local bookstore!

zonder**kidz**

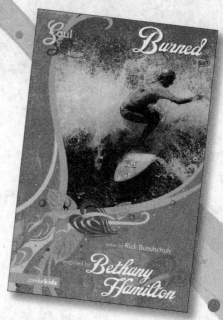

zonder**kidz**.

We want to hear from you. Please send your comments
about this book to us in care of zreview@zondervan.com. Thank you.

Grand Rapids, MI 49530
www.zonderkidz.com

ZONDERVAN.com/
AUTHORTRACKER
follow your favorite authors